GABRIELLE BLONDELL

NUMB

First published 2020 by Hey Homosapiens Press
www.heyhomosapiens.com
heyhomosapiens@gmail.com
Copyright © Gabrielle Blondell 2020

This is a work of fiction. Names, characters and incidents are a product of the author's imagination.

Cover design and typesetting by Nada Backovic
Cover photographs by iStockphotos
Author photo by Brad Delaney at Bradkay Photographix
Printed in Australia by IngramSpark

ISBN
978-0-6488790-0-8 (paperback)
987-0-6488790-1-5 (e-book)

A catalogue record for this book is available
from the National Library of Australia

Dedication
For those who suffer

PROLOGUE

'Bubble, bubble, toil and trouble,' one would think, watching the woman grind the tiny pills to white dust – finer than dust, the stuff real dust sticks to. She runs the pestle down the inside of the mortar and finishes with a swirl in its base. This action has a ritualistic feel. Has she missed her calling, missed her epoch, and wound up respectable from a lack of options? The glass of red wine stands by her elbow. It is a rich-flavoured merlot – strong enough to hide the taint of pills, or so she is told. As for the sleeping tablets, she has heard stories. They either make one sleep soundly in one's bed or else jump from windows to meander in front of trains. Tonight, she will leave the sliding door open in case the latter is his preference.

THE CRACK OF IT

A woman stood in the long paddock gazing at an enormous tree. A farmer too, but his gaze was directed so far, it had turned inward. If not for the hump of a small hill between them, he would be staring at the woman's left cheek. As it was, only the cows, which ambled down the paddock to the shade of the tree, were aware of the two. If both the farmer and the woman had set out with a purpose, they were long since forgotten. The woman was preoccupied with breathing, taking in large lungfuls of air. While there was no intention to touch the gods in any way, this is what had occurred. She was, at this moment, blank. Not so, the gun-toting farmer. In his mind, he had travelled far and was knee-deep in a South-East Asian rice paddy, the ghost water around his legs warm as blood.

The sound of a car disturbed them both. It brought the approaching cows back to the woman and an awareness of the dry, hard earth to the farmer. He strode down the hill into the dip where rainwater had accumulated and turned the grass rice-paddy green. Then, he mounted the small hill before him. From its crest, he could see the woman turn away from the tree toward the sound of the vehicle she could not yet see. He watched as she waded through the long grass toward the old farmhouse and the overgrown dirt track which lay before it. The farmer shifted his attention to the red car approaching in the distance. He lay flat between the tussocks of grass, pressed the rifle against his cheek, and sighted the car through his scope. It was low-slung and struggling over the heap of dirt and grass in the centre of the rutted track. The farmer lowered the gun and watched the drawing together of the two parties – the woman and the car. His mind plotted the point of their intersection. He watched, still as a stone, as the woman climbed awkwardly through the barbed-wire fence and the car drew to a stop outside the farmhouse. He looked on as the back doors burst open and two boys, one small and round and one tall and long-limbed, crossed the distance to the woman. The farmer saw them merge. Only then did he rise to his feet and move on.

⁜

Fiona stood on the verandah of the dilapidated farmhouse. Her gaze still rested on the tree in the paddock. She thought it might be bigger than an elephant, possibly taller than a tipped-up whale. If it weren't for the trunk, the farmhouse at her back would fit under its canopy. Beyond it, there was a grouping of smaller trees, fringing the unseen creek. She supposed this, but she couldn't know for sure. She knew a creek bordered one edge of the property. That was all. She thought of gravity. The gentle downward slope of the paddock extended to the line of trees, making it possible a creek might lie there. She would take a walk later with an easy diversion past the tree. She would stand right under it, be encompassed by it, no longer an outsider.

There was a rattle behind her, followed by, 'Jesus, Fi! This door is a nightmare!'

Fiona yanked on the screen door to release her sister.

'It may need to be rehung. It's a hinge problem, don't you think?' Julia said, bursting onto the verandah.

'Yes.' Fiona didn't shift her gaze from the tree.

'Perhaps Graham could look at it. I remember him doing something with a door at home. Should I ask him?'

Fiona nodded.

Julia placed her hands on her hips. 'Well anyway, I think I've found a great spot for the sofa.'

'Thanks. That's important.' Fiona smiled at her sister then.

'Yes, it is.' But Julia didn't smile back. Instead, she focused on the weed-ridden garden in the foreground and the tree beyond. Fiona felt the air around them grow still and heavy.

'Are you sure about this?' Julia asked.

'Yes.'

They stood there for a time, looking out from the verandah. Fiona felt her older sister's presence at her shoulder, right where she had always been.

'What about your work?' Julia asked. 'Won't it suffer with you being this far out?'

'It's okay. I can do a lot from here. Just a couple of meetings in town each week. It will be good.'

'And the kids?' Julia's voice broke, as if she might cry.

The sound of Fiona's sons floated to her from the yard. She leaned over the railing and glimpsed Hugh as he jogged back behind the house. Amongst the bushes bordering the side fence, Lochie crouched sifting dark soil through his fingers.

Fiona knew they were here because she was here and because they trusted her.

Julia turned away from the yard and placed her hands on Fiona's shoulders. 'It's just that it's seventeen years of marriage,' she whispered.

Fiona felt the crack of it. A severing had occurred. She could not go back, even if she wanted to. She wanted more than anything for Julia to leave now, so she could go to the tree and examine the trunk and feel the cool air and then wander down to the river she wasn't sure was there. She knew she had to wait. There was a rhythm to such weighty conversations. They stopped time and the pause must be given its due.

'Do you remember us back then?' Julia prodded. 'You'd finished high school and I was in second year. We'd just had that big bong when Richard walked in. God, we were off our tits.'

The room is classic university dorm with a communal living space. Art prints are thumb-tacked crookedly to walls. The furniture is pine and spare and so uncomfortable any lounging, TV-watching or bong-smoking is done sitting on the floor. Fiona is giddy from her big sister's invitation to join her and, while she has already arrived, she doesn't feel it is real yet. The bong is her first ever and that will also take time, better experienced in retrospect.

A figure appears slouched against the door jamb. He is a hazy presence through the smoke both inside and outside her head. Richard appears to glide toward them. He takes the bong and the cigarette lighter from her hands and says something to Julia. Fiona thinks it is, 'How irresponsible, Jules.' He smiles to show he is joking. It is right then, in the way he singles her out for his concern, that she starts wanting him.

✳

It was cool and dark under the giant tree. With its trunk at her back and two of its buttress roots twisting out on either side of her, Fiona was supported enough to feel nothing. It was the prickling of goosebumps on her bare arms which brought her back.

As much as she fought it in public, this tendency to drift off happened often. She would come to at her desk or waiting in line somewhere or in her car at the traffic lights and not know where she had been. She wondered if this was what a nervous breakdown felt like. But then, no, a breakdown couldn't feel this good. The world had taken to vanishing. It was as if her brain said, 'That's enough now,' and drew the blinds. Fiona didn't feel distress in these moments. She felt it when the world came back. Her hands shook as her heart bore the shock of it. Like all travellers in space, it was the re-entry which proved the most challenging.

'Mum!'

Fiona heard Lochie before she saw the dark outline of his stocky little body against the setting sun.

'Mum!'

She stilled her breathing and clasped her quivering hands in her lap as he approached. His excitement reached out ahead of him but stopped just short of her.

'We found a creek. It's awesome! You have to come see it.'

'I will. I'll do it tomorrow,' she said. 'It's getting too late now.'

Lochie's attention skipped on. 'We found an old chook shed too and Hugh reckons there used to be a veggie garden around the side of the house.'

'Really?'

Lochie planted his feet in front of her and placed his hands firmly on his hips. 'I think it's going to be cool living here.'

Fiona had rented the house out of desperation. It had a roof and walls. That was enough. She had not expected them to like it. On her first and only visit, the junior estate agent engaged in none of the usual banter. Instead, he stood in the centre of the sitting room, battered, she imagined, by memories of past rental applicants who had walked in and straight back out again. It was she who asked the questions.

'So, three bedrooms, yes?'

'Two and a half,' he said, pointing toward the sleep-out on the enclosed back verandah.

And that was that. She said yes because the rent was low, and it was someplace else. The estate agent ended their deal, smiling and shaking her hand. He led her out of the front door to the verandah. It was there he pointed out the finer detail.

'It's owned by an old farmer over the hill,' he said. 'And there's a creek on one of the boundaries. Quite nice, really,' he nodded, enthusiastic now that the deal was done.

'Could we have chickens?' Lochie asked, standing above her under the tree. 'Hugh wants some, and maybe we could fix up the veggie garden too?'

Lochie reached out his hands to pull Fiona to her feet. She pushed herself forward with his help and for a moment their faces were only centimetres apart. It reminded her of a time when Lochie could sit on her lap, his face close enough to read through the skin. She saw anticipation there now ... and hope. Fiona was struck by it. She wanted to feel as though she had gone somewhere with a purpose. She wanted it to mean something, but she was afraid it didn't.

She followed Lochie up the hill toward the house knowing, of all feelings, this one predominated. Things, which used to matter, didn't now. There was no one watching to see if she got it right.

She was still preoccupied when Lochie came to a halt in front of her.

'Look,' Lochie whispered, pointing ahead to where the slope steepened beyond the house and formed a small knoll.

Fiona made out the silhouette of a tall, thin man against the lowering sun. He was staring beyond them into the distance with what looked like a gun resting at an angle on his hip. Fiona turned and followed his gaze back toward the tree. Cows were gathering there, rocking themselves into lying positions. She raised a hand to wave hello and saw the abrupt shift in his posture. The gun came down and she was sure she heard the thump of the rifle butt against the ground. Then she supposed she saw the smallest of nods in their direction, a tiny tip of the head before the farmer raised the gun onto his shoulder and disappeared over the rise.

'Weird,' said Lochie, his eyes big.

'Not really,' answered Fiona.

'But he had a gun.'

'Well, farmers do have guns, Lochie. They have to protect their stock from predators – dingoes and such.'

'Should we get a gun?'

'We are not farmers.'

'We'll have chooks. Dingoes like chooks too, don't they?' Lochie asked.

'No,' Fiona lied.

They continued on.

This time it was Fiona who stopped. 'Where's your brother?'

'Dunno. Probably gone back to the house,' Lochie said, still trudging up the hill ahead of her.

At the front gate, Fiona heard a hollow knocking coming from around the side of the house. She found Hugh, his shirt discarded, with an old hoe in his hands. On either side of him were piles of cracked garden edging and a cleared line where the edging must have been. Fiona followed the curve of it, and saw it formed a circle with spokes to divide the garden into segments.

Hugh stopped working and posed beside his hoe, his chest thrust out, one bicep clenched. 'It's cool, hey?'

She almost didn't know him. Something had happened. A gap had formed between the boy she knew and the young man she was yet to meet. 'Yes, it is cool. Where did you get the hoe?'

'Did Lochie tell you about the chook pen?'

'Yes,' she said, trying hard to read him.

'It was in there. A shovel too.'

Fiona nodded, 'Right.' Her mind drifted in and out of the feathered leaves of the pepper tree behind her son.

Hugh shifted his position. 'So, Mum? Can we put in a vegetable garden and get chickens for eggs? We might as well. It's all here.'

It was, but even as it was laid out in front of her, Fiona couldn't see far enough ahead. 'I'll need to ask permission first.'

Hugh shook his head and frowned at her. 'Why?'

'Because we don't own the land, Hugh. The farmer does.'

Fiona lingered out of Hugh's sight and listened as the hoe struck the earth again. Her attention wandered to the spot where the farmer had stood on the hill. She watched the sun travel down, quicker now that it was almost home.

❋

Inside the house, there was much to do. Boxes teetered behind the sofa, but Fiona didn't care. They could wait. Indefinitely, perhaps. She walked past them to the kitchen at the back of the house. There, she sat at an old table, pushed against one wall to allow passage to the back verandah. The evidence of this was visible on the curling linoleum floor. Two grime-filled gouges showed where the leading legs of the table had dug in.

Fiona heard creaking footsteps and the swing of the back door. It was Hugh coming in from the sleep-out, a narrow room with louvered windows and a floor which sloped away from the rest of the house as if it might disconnect itself and wander off.

She realised some time had passed since Hugh had ceased to hoe the garden. He had showered. Part of her mind had recorded that, the cessation of the heavy thump of metal on soil, the running water in the bathroom, the hammering in the pipes. Since then, an impenetrable darkness had fallen. It was unlike anything in the city. It crowded at the windows now, looking in at her.

'Mum?'

'Yes?'

'Don't you think we should cook something to eat?' Hugh said this as if he were breaking bad news.

'Yes, yes. Of course.' Fiona drew herself up. 'Yes. What about eggs? We could have them scrambled with some bacon, if you like?'

'That would be great. Breakfast for dinner.'

'Yes.'

Hugh leaned against the tiny kitchen bench with his arms folded, bigger than she had ever remembered him. Closer too, now Richard was gone.

'I'll find a whisk and the frypan, if you get the eggs and cream,' she said.

Lochie crouched behind the television in the sitting room. He peaked out at her with a bunch of cables in his hand. 'Just setting things up,' he said.

'Thank goodness for that,' Fiona said. She picked out a frypan from a box marked *pans* and found a whisk in another marked *implements*. She saw the handwriting again as she folded the cardboard flaps back down and tried to work out if it were Julia's or her own. It hardly seemed to matter, except that these tiny facts anchored her.

'Mum, are you okay?'

Lochie emerged from behind the television and stood in front of the sofa staring at her.

'Yes, yes. I'm fine. Scrambled eggs in ten minutes, okay? And I want you at the kitchen table to eat it.'

Lochie screwed up his face. 'Why can't I have my dinner on the sofa just this once? Come on, Mum.'

'I said come to the table, Lochie, and I meant it.' Honestly, she didn't care. Her drawing of lines was indiscriminate now.

Lochie positioned himself on the sofa with remote control in hand. 'No. I don't want to!'

Fiona heard the footsteps in the hall.

'Lochie, you will sit at the table, like Mum says!' Hugh was beside her.

Fiona heard Richard in his voice.

'I don't have to do what you tell me!' Lochie yelled at Hugh.

Before Fiona could stop him, Hugh launched himself over the back of the sofa and landed on top of his brother.

Fiona ran to them. 'Stop it. Stop it, both of you!' She pulled at Hugh's arm which had curled itself around Lochie's neck. 'We can't have this here. Do you understand? Not ever!'

Hugh released Lochie abruptly and left the room. She heard the door slam and the sleep-out louvres rattle. Big tears gathered in Lochie's eyes, dripped and ran down his cheeks. 'I hate him,' he sniffed.

'You don't hate him, Lochie. He's your brother.'

'Yes, I do.' Lochie stood, walked up the hall to his room and closed the door behind him.

Fiona cooked bacon and scrambled eggs, hoping the smell would coax them out again, but it didn't. She wished she could talk to them like she used to, but they were too raw now. Their anger was so close to the surface. Hers too.

GRAVES OF
DEAD DOGS

Hugh and Lochie sat at the breakfast table staring off into the distance like estranged aristocrats. Fiona pretended not to notice, but in the confines of the car their silence was oppressive. 'I'm going into the office today, but I'll be back in time to pick you up, okay?' She said this as she drew the car to a stop outside the school bus stop.

Neither boy answered her.

Fiona felt a string pull tight inside her. 'Okay?' she demanded again.

They responded by silently exiting the car and leaving her to it. Fiona's lungs spasmed and her throat contracted, as if she might sob. Of all things, she needed solidarity between the three of them. The cracks were deep. She knew it, but for now she wanted to plaster over them and imagine they weren't there. Let them pretend there were no divisions between them. Just for a time. Fiona drove away, leaving Lochie and Hugh standing by the side of the road staring down it in opposite directions.

Padma squinted through her reading glasses as Fiona walked past the front desk. Her eyes widened when she recognised Fiona. 'It's so good to see you!' she gushed. 'It's been a while.'

Fiona paused. 'Yes, it has. It's good to see you too,' she said, making to move off again.

'So, how's the tree change?' Padma asked after her.

'Pardon?' Fiona stopped again.

'The tree change. Steph told me about you moving out of town.' Padma studied Fiona. 'How is it?'

'Oh, it's fine. It's good, very peaceful,' Fiona answered. 'Is Steph in?'

'She had to pop out for a bit, but she shouldn't be long,' Padma said. 'There's some background here for you to look over.' She shuffled through the papers on her desk while Fiona stood limply by. 'Here it is,' she said, passing her a file. 'Hey, are you okay?'

'I'm fine,' Fiona said, forcing a smile. 'I'll wait in the conference room, shall I?'

'Sure.'

Fiona dropped her notebook and papers onto the conference table and watched them slide across the glossy surface. All interactions were difficult now. It was as if she didn't know how to be with people, even Padma and Steph, who she had known for such a long time. She closed her eyes and took a deep breath.

'So, is country living turning out to be the bore we suspected it to be?'

Fiona's eyes snapped open as her editor entered the room and sat opposite her.

'I'm liking it, actually,' Fiona answered.

'That's great. I am happy for you, even though I think you and that husband of yours are crazy. I mean who leaves a perfectly good city to go play in the mud?'

Fiona smiled steadily.

'Have you had a chance to go through that lot?' Steph inclined her head toward the background material on the table between them.

'Not yet,' Fiona replied.

'Okay. I'm still keen for the 'Bullying in the Workplace' feature and there's plenty of stuff for you to go on with. It needs to be the first thing we slot in.' Steph pulled out her diary, a large hard-backed, dog-eared thing, upholstered in post-it notes. She flipped it open and made a note.

'Okay,' Fiona agreed. 'I'll see who I can talk to over at Fair Work Nation.'

'Good. I think a deadline of the 15th should work, don't you?'

It wasn't a question. Fiona wrote the date in her notebook.

'Okay, what's next?' Steph consulted her diary. 'There's Gordon Watts.'

'Who?' Fiona asked.

'We are overdue for a gender piece, particularly since the release of the James Report. I'll get Padma to run you off a copy.' Steph made a note on another post-it and stuck it to the front cover of her diary. 'Watts has some interesting things to say about gender inequality and he's the keynote speaker at the organisational psychology conference next month.'

'Okay. For the July issue, right?'

'Yup. I'll get Padma to get you entry to the conference and you can scout me some more stories while you are there.'

Steph opened her diary and flipped to a page which was more ink than paper and indecipherable to anyone other than Padma and herself.

Fiona's head was beginning to throb.

'Are you okay?' Steph was staring at her.

'Yes, yes. I'm fine,' she said.

'I don't want you going bonkers on me and taking up subsistence farming or knitting goat-hair sweaters.'

'No. I promise. No farming. No sweaters.'

'Right, then. That's plenty to go on with, I think.' Steph stood and picked up her diary. 'I have to go, but I'll see you next week.'

'Sure.'

Fiona waited until Steph had swept out of the conference room before she pulled her mobile phone from her bag and dialled.

'Hello. Is that Happy Valley Realty?'

'Yes. How can we help?' The voice was crisp.

'I'm a tenant in the old farmhouse out on Possum Creek Road. I wanted to –'

'Oh, yes. I'll transfer you to property management. Please hold the line.'

Fiona waited.

'Hello?' This voice was tentative. 'Is there a problem, Mrs Lees?'

'No, there's no problem.'

'Oh good. That's good, isn't it?'

'Yes, I guess so.'

'How can I help you then?' The voice was calmer now, a deeper register. Fiona was reminded of Hugh.

'Mrs Lees?'

'Oh yes. It's about the garden –'

'Yes, I know it's a bit of a mess, but the vendor refuses to pay our gardening fee. I thought I told you this on your visit,' the agent said.

'No, I don't think you did, but I'm not ringing to complain.'

'Right, that's a relief, isn't it?'

'I suppose it is. I would like permission to put in a vegetable garden and keep some chickens, that's all. I didn't want to bother the owner.'

'Yes right. Alick's a bit of an old character, isn't he?'

Fiona saw the silhouette of the man on the hill with the gun jutting from his hip. 'Should I be worried about him?'

'No, not at all,' the agent replied, quickly.

The pause between them lengthened. 'So, will you ask the farmer if we could keep chickens and fix the gardens?'

'There is no need, Mrs Lees,' he said. 'It's in the paperwork. There will be no objections to keeping animals or fixing gardens. According to this –'

Fiona heard papers rustling.

'– you could put in a zoo and it wouldn't be a problem.' He spluttered in her ear at his own joke.

'Thank you, Mr –'

'Call me, Troy.'

'Thank you, Troy.'

❅

She and Hugh worked steadily in the garden. They moved side-by-side on their hands and knees, plucking the last of the weeds in a kind of rhythm, a swaying dance leaning this way and that, with arms reaching. They spoke little. There was no need. Fiona felt a spurt of gratitude. She had been sure she was losing him. There had been many times in recent days when she had caught him looking at her and in the tilt of his chin, she had seen his judgement. But today was different. She knew something unique to them both had been preserved. If she could just hold on to it, they might always know each other.

Hugh was returning from another trip to the compost bin when he said, 'I think I want to study horticulture when I leave school. I really like working outside. Doing things like this, you know?' He dropped to his knees beside her to resume his weeding.

Fiona stretched out her back and smiled at Hugh. 'Yes, I've noticed.'

The change in their lives was fundamental and yet Hugh had taken it on. He was leaning into his future and this set off a tremor inside her. She could not think of opportunities because she could not think at all.

'So, can I? Do horticulture?' Hugh asked her, excited now. 'I know you thought I'd do something more ... office-like.'

'I did,' she said, studying Hugh's high forehead, the sweep of it down toward his serious brows.

'I'm not copping out,' he said, finally.

'Don't worry,' Fiona said, returning to her weeding. 'People know the difference between someone who really wants to do things and someone who is pretending.'

'You mean, like Dad?'

Fiona stilled herself. When she looked up, Hugh was staring at her. 'No. No, I didn't mean your father. I meant people in general.' She looked down at the soil once more.

She knew Hugh was watching her. She heard her mobile phone shrill inside the farmhouse, but she didn't move.

'It's okay, Mum. Lochie and I know the score. We know what he's like.' Hugh's voice was soft.

Was this how they would begin to talk of it? After so much silence, she thought she had more time. She thought she would be the one to speak first. The phone ceased its ringing and Lochie's voice was muffled inside the house.

Fiona still didn't move. The void inside her head was a creaking, echoing place, so very different from the world outside of it. When she finally raised her head, Hugh had bent to his weeding again. 'I'd better go see who called,' she said, standing and brushing the soil from her knees.

Inside the farmhouse, Fiona found Lochie talking excitedly into the phone.

'And, Grandma, he's got a gun!'

Fiona reached for the telephone.

'Mum's here, Grandma.' Lochie passed it over.

Fiona pressed the phone to her ear. 'Hello, Mum.'

'Oh Fiona! Lochie tells me the farmer carries a gun,' Gwendolyn said in a voice designed to carry across auditoriums.

'Yes Mum, the farmer carries a gun,' Fiona said, frowning at Lochie, who took this opportunity to leave the room. 'We are fine.'

'But a gun, Fiona ... a gun! What sort of person in this day and age carries a gun?'

'Farmers do, Mum.' And policemen and security guards and psychopaths.

Gwendolyn continued. 'I mean, what about the children? I really don't understand you anymore.'

Fiona took a deep breath. 'A farmer with a gun, who is only protecting his cows, is no one's problem. Not mine or yours.'

Gwendolyn sighed. 'It's okay, darling. There is no need to be dramatic. I just want you to be careful. '

A silence fell between them. Their conversations were often punctuated by such silences.

'Was there a reason for your call?' Fiona asked.

'Oh yes, that's right! I rang to remind you of opening night this Friday. Please bring the boys. I know they'll enjoy it!'

Fiona had forgotten. 'Of course, Mum. We will be there.'

'Okay darling, I'll see you then.'

Fiona found Lochie on the sofa in the lounge room. He looked up as she entered.

'We need to go to Grandma's opening night on Friday evening.'

'Okay.'

'And go get Hugh. It's nearly dinner time.'

Lochie swung himself off the sofa and was almost out of the door when Fiona called to him.

'And Lochie?'

'Yep?'

'Stop telling your Grandmother about the farmer and his gun, okay?'

'Okay, Mum.'

*

Julia sits alongside her, arranging her own costume. There is makeup smudged on on her face made to look like dirt and eleven-year-old Fiona knows her own face is the same. A large frame of painted, city buildings rolls by. They too look like buildings without being buildings. The windows don't open and neither do all but one of the doors. That door flaps as the structure passes. It is through there Fiona will exit after she has said her one line: 'Yes sir.'

'Do you know what to do?' Julia asks her in a tone which implies she couldn't possibly.

'Yes sir,' Fiona replies.

Julia, a veteran of three of their mother's plays, sighs. 'You know you can't stuff this up, Fi, so you better take it seriously. What about the other kids who really wanted the role?'

Fiona hadn't known there were any.

'It's a great opportunity. It's how I started, you know,' her sister says.

Julia is only three years older than Fiona. 'You want to do it, don't you?'

Fiona knows Julia asks because she is protecting her. She nods enthusiastically, so her sister will know it is true. She has grown into the wanting of it.

'We have to go side-stage now,' her sister says, and she takes Fiona by the wrist. Fiona doesn't wrestle her arm free. Suddenly, she is scared. She wants her sister to drag her about and never let her go. They weave their way past props and people. Fiona stumbles onward. She can't feel her feet, only the pressure of Julia's grip and the pull on her arm. She considers if her legs were to stop walking, she would not know. She would fall face-first onto the floor and be genuinely dirty. She wills herself to step consciously.

Julia looks back at her. 'What's wrong with you?' she asks, still dragging her. 'You look like a puppet.'

'Sorry,' Fiona mumbles.

They stop in the wings. It is silent there. Fiona watches as a man gestures to a woman across the stage in the opposite wing. She sees the woman's face change from worry to a broad rigid smile as she steps out under the brilliant spotlights.

Julia turns Fiona to face her. 'It's all right, you know. Everyone gets nervous,' she whispers.

Fiona looks up at Julia. 'Are you nervous?'

'Packing shit,' says Julia.

Fiona giggles and repeats the words. 'Packing shit.'

'You know Mum will be down there in the front row, scared out of her mind.'

'Really?' Fiona asks.

'Yep.'

'Okay.'

'Are you ready?'

'Yep,' Fiona says, and she is.

The gesturing man is beside them now. He smiles. 'Ready?' he whispers.

Her sister nods for both of them.

He taps their shoulders and Julia steps out onto the stage.

'Go,' he urges Fiona.

Fiona follows. The spotlights blind her momentarily. Beyond them, the audience is a gaping mouth ready to swallow her. Fiona feels Julia tug at her. She hears her sister's voice. 'This is my younger brother, Charlie.'

Fiona pulls her attention away from the black maw beyond the footlights and tries to focus on Julia and the 'policeman', who is really a cash register operator at the local supermarket. Fiona stares at him. He has a pimple which looks like a snow-covered mountain poking through his stage makeup.

This tiny alp jumps and wobbles when he says, 'Charlie, can you fetch Miss Watson down?'

Fiona has heard the line said so many times, it is no longer a question. It has become individual words without meaning.

'Charlie – can – you – fetch – Miss – Watson – down?' he tries again.

Fiona stares at the pimple.

Julia answers for her. 'Yes, you'll do that won't you, Charlie?'

She steps in close and looks into Fiona's face, urging her to say something. They are not there, those words. 'Yes sir,' has fled with the real world. Her sister clasps Fiona's arm and pulls her across the stage. She hears the audience giggle as they disappear through the flapping door.

A heavy drop of rain smacked Fiona on the forehead as she and the boys mounted the stairs of the Performing Arts Centre. Another raindrop splashed on her arm and then another. The small group of theatre-goers hurried past them to get inside.

In the second row of the auditorium, Fiona's father stood waving a programme to attract their attention. Julia and her husband, Graham, were already in their seats.

'Sorry we're late, Dad,' Fiona said.

'Well, it's a much longer drive now, I guess,' Stuart said, wrapping both arms around Fiona and resting his chin on top of her head. For the briefest of moments, Fiona thought she might cry.

'Where's Mum?' Fiona asked.

'Your mother's backstage,' he said, still holding her. 'You know how nervous she gets.'

Fiona nodded.

Her father released her and greeted the boys. 'He's getting big,' he said, watching Hugh find his seat.

'He is,' Fiona agreed.

'So, how are you?' he asked, holding her at arm's length and studying her.

'I'm good,' Fiona answered, returning his stare.

He pulled her in close again. 'We both know you're lying,' he whispered before letting her go.

Fiona slipped in beside her sister and her brother-in-law. She smiled at Julia and Julia squeezed her elbow. Graham leaned across his wife and patted Fiona's knee.

'I hear you've taken to the country life,' he said.

It was such an odd thing to say. She stared into his face looking for something to prick herself on, but there was nothing. Graham's face was blank, uninterested.

'Yes, we like the country very much,' she said, sounding like she was serving tea to her guests on the front lawn of her estate. Julia frowned at her, and with good reason.

Thankfully, Fiona's mother returned to the auditorium; the lights dimmed, and the curtains opened on a bedroom in Salem, 1692.

*

They do not speak. He has been alone too long. Still, he comes to her, out of the jungle, through the air and into a city uncertain of what it may become. He removes his clothes, piece by filthy piece, and takes a warm bath. As he soaks himself, he watches the rich Vietnamese fabrics waft in the windows on the smallest of breezes. He is careless about washing himself. She will come. She will wash him with a cloth and scrub him with a brush and he will sit, sometimes watching the fabric floating in the window, sometimes watching the top of her head as she bends to clean him. Later, they will retire to the bed and he will feel her body. She is small, like a bird, and he wonders how all the bodily organs can fit inside her in the same way he used to marvel at tiny finches when he was a boy.

Rain was coming, flooding rain. It was there in the silence, in the absence of birdsong, as if the bunching of the steel-coloured clouds above had a muffling effect, the low pressure like cotton wool in the ears. Alick lowered his foot from the cross-brace supporting the corner post. When the creek ran high, it found and plucked out weakness. The cross-brace did not waver.

He followed the fence line where it bordered the creek, then across the opening of the track where it met the road. There was another entrance to the property on the high side, near his house, but he kept that to himself. He slipped through the deep shadow of the camphor laurel trees until he was across from the farmhouse.

Something was different. Not the house. It was the same as it had always been. Older, less cared for, but resilient despite him. No, not that. As he scanned the surrounds, the first, heavy drops fell. He crept closer still, around the side of the house toward his mother's garden. He could see it now. The paths were cleared, the old vegetable garden weeded, the broken edging heaped into cairns, like the graves of dead dogs.

THE GLORY OF ANONYMITY

In the days that followed, the rain continued to fall. At the farm, the creek rose beyond the tree line. It crossed the road, blocking it, and the world shrunk to three square kilometres of flattish ground and the same again of steep, barely traversable country. Fiona was drawn to the floodwaters. She stood for long stretches, mesmerised by its hurry, its impatience, its blind boiling around the large tree trunks as if they didn't matter.

She had retreated to the verandah when Steph rang.

'How's it going with the bullying feature?' Steph asked immediately.

'It's great,' Fiona lied. She watched a large tree trunk bob its way across the paddock. 'Hey, I don't know if I'll get into the office this week,' she said.

'So, is it raining down your way?' Steph asked. 'It's cats and dogs here. The traffic is such rubbish. Some arse decided it was a wonderful idea to run into another arse on the Story

Bridge this morning. Just freaking fantastic! I missed my meeting with the powers that be.'

'That's too bad,' Fiona said, smiling. Steph was irreverent with those whose job it was to manage her.

Fiona heard a rattle and the faulty screen door flew open. Hugh spilled out onto the verandah.

'Hang on, Steph,' she said. She called after Hugh who was already halfway down the stairs. 'Where are you going?'

'For a run,' he said.

'In this weather?'

He stopped and scowled. 'It's just rain, Mum.'

'Okay then. Where's Lochie?'

'He's in the lounge, messing about with the digital camera.'

'Right. Well, be careful near the creek. Don't go in, will you?'

'I'm not stupid.'

Fiona held his gaze. 'No, you're not.'

'They are growing up, aren't they?' Steph's voice was tinny through the phone receiver.

'Yes, they are,' Fiona said, watching Hugh jog down the path.

They were silent with each other as the rain fell. Fiona felt swaddled by it, the tiny farmhouse, Steph's breath in her ear. Could she tell Steph about her life, about everything? They had known each other for a long time.

'Are you still there?'

'Sure,' Fiona said. 'Hey, I better go though. There are interviews to set up.'

'Right. Keep me updated once you've spoken to Fair Work Nation,' Steph said.

'Yep. Absolutely.'

Fiona read through the background material Steph had given her. She located the name of the media liaison at the employment advocacy service and dialled the number.

A woman answered. 'Hello, Vivian speaking. How may I help you?'

'Hi, this is Fiona Lees from *In Business*. Could I speak with Michael Green, please?'

'Certainly. I'll check to see if he is available.'

'Thanks.' Fiona waited.

'Hello, Fiona. I don't believe we've met. May I call you Fiona?' The voice was friendly.

'Fiona is fine. So, Michael, we are doing a feature on workplace bullying and I'd like to talk to one of your advocates, if that's okay? I want to get a sense of not just how prevalent it is, but how it affects the individual, if you know what I mean?'

'Sure. Statistics are bloodless, aren't they?'

'Yes, they can be.' Fiona waited. She allowed the small silence between them to grow.

'Okay, then,' Green said, jumping into the space. 'Leave it with me.'

'Thanks Michael. I have a deadline for the 15th.'

'Right. I'll get back to you.'

Fiona was thinking about lunch and whether she should begin to conserve food when Hugh ran up the front stairs like a wet dog.

'Go have a warm shower and I'll be onto lunch soon,' she said.

Hugh disappeared inside the house and Fiona saved Green's number to her contacts list. Just as she was pushing herself out of her chair, Hugh rushed back onto the verandah.

'Where's Lochie?' he asked.

'Why?' Fiona could feel his urgency. 'Wasn't he in the lounge room when you left?'

Hugh shrugged. 'Well, he's not now and he's not in his room either. He's not in the house at all.'

＊

First, it had been the woman. He'd come across her when checking the creek pump. She was standing still, staring into the floodwaters. Then, he saw the older boy running along the edge of the swollen creek in the bottom paddock. The old tension had resurfaced. He watched as the boy hurdled a large branch pushed aside by the floodwater. He did this without effort, without breaking his stride. Alick frowned and turned over the tractor's engine.

The old farmhouse had lain empty for almost a year, since the last tenants had moved on. For the most part, Alick was ambivalent. He just hadn't gotten around to pulling it down. 'A house should be lived in,' his mother said when families started walking off the land back in the '50s. He could hear her now, as he watched the spray kick up behind the boy's running shoes. She would have been happy about the children. There had been no children on the property since he was one. As for him, he liked children no better than he liked anyone else. Alick engaged the clutch in the old tractor and it lurched into gear. The boy came out of the tree line as he moved toward higher ground. Not for the first time, he thought he should leave the place vacant and watch from a distance as it returned to the soil.

Alick is hoeing two large segments of his mother's garden. The frosts are almost over and the seed potatoes can be planted without fear. The hoe strikes deep, powered by his anger and resentment because he suspects there is a world out there and his father is determined to make a farmer of him. It is the curse of an only child. It was fine, Alick thinks, when families were large. The chances were high that one among them would gladly take up the job. But there is only him.

The problem, as he sees it, is he could be a farmer, but he could be a lot of other things. He could explore the world and be invisible at last. He could walk down a street, weaving in and out of the crowds, and not have to say 'Good day' to anyone. They would need nothing, not even a nod of his head. But here, he must be always mindful of those he meets, for he has met them before and will go on meeting them over and over until he leaves this place. It's unnatural, he thinks – the way incest is unnatural. The thought is so captivating he ceases his hoeing and devotes his full attention to it.

'Alick, those seed potatoes won't plant themselves,' his mother yells from the kitchen window, but Alick doesn't hear her. He stands motionless, all outward movement conserved as he dreams of anonymity.

Alick had finished topping up the diesel in the tractor and was about to restart the engine when he heard the whirring sound. It was a perfectly mechanical noise. His spine stiffened. He heard the sound again, closer now. A movement in the tractor's cracked side mirror caught his attention. He leaned into it and saw the younger boy from the farmhouse. The illusion caused by the broken glass disembodied the child and he appeared to float toward him. In the boy's hand was a camera. Alick watched as he raised it to his eye and pressed the shutter button. In one movement, the farmer jumped to the ground to face him. The impact on his old knees was fierce.

'What are you doing here?' he growled.

The boy halted, the camera dangling from a strap around his neck

'It's not polite to sneak up on someone, boy,' Alick said.

'I didn't mean to. I was taking photos and I saw you on the tractor, that's all.' The boy seemed prepared for an argument.

'Well then, lad, I'm not used to children and I don't particularly like them. This is a working farm, not a playground, do you understand? I better not find you down near the creek while it's in flood. I don't want to have to fish your dead body out, all right?'

The boy's eyes widened.

'Lochie!'

Alick heard the woman calling for her son. He climbed up onto the tractor and started the engine. 'Go home to your mother, lad.'

❋

'He's weird,' Lochie said, flapping the tea towel about instead of drying the dishes.

'Why? What did he say to you?' Fiona asked him, scrolling through the photos Lochie had taken on her camera. She came to the last one. The farmer stared into the lens and, while the broken glass of the tractor's side mirror drew deep lines across his already lined face, the eyes were a clear, pale blue. 'What do you mean he's weird, Lochie?'

'Just weird,' Lochie muttered, taking a dish from the drying rack and rubbing it with the tea towel. 'Anyway, I don't understand why taking a few pictures was such a big deal. Hugh's outside now, isn't he?'

'He is out checking on the garden and I know that because he told me. You said nothing to anyone and took off when the creek was in flood. We were worried,' Fiona continued to examine the photograph.

'Worried that you'd have to fish my dead body out of the creek?' Lochie asked.

Fiona started at this. Pressure built up behind her eyes. Perhaps Lochie was old enough. 'Yes,' she said, placing the camera on the kitchen table and returning to the sink to wash the rest of the dishes.

'Are you okay?' Lochie tried to peer into her face, but Fiona avoided him and looked harder into the sink. 'I'm sorry, Mum.'

Hugh came in from the garden and stared at them both. 'Everything okay?' he asked, looking from one to the other.

'Sure, we're cool, aren't we Mum?' Lochie said.

'Yep, we're cool,' Fiona said.

Her telephone rang and Lochie tossed the tea towel on the table. 'I'll get it.'

'Okay, but tell whoever it is I'll have to ring them back.' Fiona waved her soapy hands at him and returned to washing the dishes.

Lochie lifted the receiver. 'Hello? Oh ... Hi, Dad.'

Fiona fumbled with a plate in the sink and turned to face Lochie. He was already walking toward her. She could see the tension in his face. 'Yep, I'm good. Yep, Mum's here. I'll get her.' He pushed the phone into her wet hands.

Hugh and Lochie left the room. They dissolved in a manner which was as old as time. Once again, she was alone with Richard.

She could hear his impatience. 'Fiona! Fiona! Are you there?'

She could hang up on him, but even as she thought this, she raised the handset to her ear. A long drool of scummy water fell to her shoulder and slithered down her chest between her breasts. 'Yes, I'm here.'

'Good,' he said. 'I want to see my children.'

Fiona said nothing.

'I am their father and every father has a right to see their children.'

Again, she said nothing. His voice came to her from another time. She had forgotten its pull on her.

'What gives you the right to move them without telling me? A father should know where his children are.'

His insistence drew her in close. She knew this conversation. Humiliation would follow.

'You want your space?' he asked with heavy sarcasm.

She couldn't answer him.

'Well, sweetheart, you can have all the space you want, but I want to see my kids.'

Not true, she screamed inside her head.

'Look, Fiona. Let's be adults about this. Both you and I know those kids will be back with me within six months. You won't be able to cope.'

Bile reared up from the pit of Fiona's belly.

'I'm worried about your state of mind,' Richard said. 'You are not rational. You fed me pills for fuck's sake. You are in no condition to look after the boys by yourself.'

Fiona hung up and vomited halfway down the hall to the bathroom. She sat for some time on the floor in the hall beside her own vomit and the boys materialised again. Lochie edged his way toward her and sat next to her. Hugh slouched in the door frame leading to the sitting room.

'What did he want?' Hugh asked.

Fiona didn't answer. There was no language for this.

Hugh left the hall and brought back a roll of paper towel and disinfectant. He crouched beside her and started to clean up her vomit.

'Don't,' she said. 'I'll do it.' But he kept rubbing on the patch of floor, tearing and wiping until the roll was finished and the floor was clean. Then, he sat down opposite them and stared at her, every part of him still.

'What did he want?' he asked again.

Fiona could see by his eyes he already knew. 'He wants to see you.'

'No!' he yelled, pushing himself to his feet. 'I don't want to see him. I don't ever want to see him.'

Fiona saw his fear, and this should have stopped her.

'He is your father, Hugh. He has a right,' she said, rising to speak face-to-face with her son.

Hugh screamed, 'He is not a father! He has no rights! Look at what he did to you, how he treated us!'

He was pacing the length of the hall now, feeding his anger. Lochie cringed beside her, as Hugh strode back toward them.

'You only want us to see him because it will take the heat off you! I thought things had changed, but they haven't. You still do what he wants.' Hugh spat this at her and grabbed for Lochie. 'Don't you see him, Lochie. Don't you dare. She doesn't know what she is doing.'

Lochie pulled away. 'Yes, she does!' he yelled back.

Hugh grabbed him again and pulled him close. 'No, she fucking-well doesn't!'

Fiona felt the tears come. She had so much to be sorry for and she wanted to tell Hugh this, but before she could, he had released Lochie, grabbed his runners and was out of the front door.

That night, Fiona bolted the front and back doors of the farmhouse for the first time since they had moved in because the floodwaters were receding.

THE DEAD COW DAY

Overnight, Lochie developed a fever and stiffness in his neck, but there was little she could do until the local doctor's surgery opened. She hovered over Lochie while he slept. Please let him be okay, she whispered. It could be flu, but then it could be something else. Meningococcal disease, perhaps. Her mind ran in circles. It's nothing. It's life-threatening. It's nothing.

She heard the screen door slam and slumped down onto Lochie's bed. Hugh's rage over Richard's phone call cowed her. She flinched as she heard his hoe strike the earth, imagining the sparks flying from the broken edging as slithers of anger. What had happened so many times before had happened again. Something in her lost balance and fell where Richard was concerned. Fiona lay her palm on Lochie's forehead.

'Australian Spotted Fever,' the doctor said.
    'What?'

He rolled Lochie's head to one side and pointed to a small, angry wound behind his ear. 'I suspect he has had a paralysis tick,' he said. 'Sometimes these ticks carry with them a bacterial parasite which can cause Australian Spotted Fever.' The doctor's voice was perfectly modulated, each word designed to becalm.

'Oh. So, a parasite on a parasite?' Fiona said, her voice ragged in comparison.

'Yes. I know it sounds weird, but that's about it,' he chuckled.

'Are you sure it's not meningococcus?' she challenged him.

'Absolutely. Meningococcus progresses much faster than this and the presence of the tick bite, the recent weather and this being prime tick country leads me to think Australian Spotted Fever is our best bet.' The doctor smiled again in an encouraging fashion. 'A blood test will confirm it, but in the meantime, I'll write out a prescription for an antibiotic, okay?'

'Yes. Thank you.' Despite herself, she was relieved. Tears appeared from nowhere and Fiona turned away, as if to study a chart on women's reproductive health.

'Are you all right?' the doctor asked.

'Yes, yes. I'm fine.'

A nurse came and took Lochie's blood. The doctor studied Fiona across his desk. 'You must be the new tenants in Alick's farmhouse. Harry told me he'd rented the old place again.'

Fiona disguised her alarm. She had meant for them to disappear. 'Who's Harry?'

'Local livestock vet. Knows everyone. Small town. You know how it goes. He's the only one who sees Alick anymore.'

'Alick?' She looked toward Lochie on the consultation bed. The nurse was writing on the vial of blood.

'The farmer who owns the property,' he answered.

'Oh yes, of course,' she said, redirecting her attention to the doctor.

'Old Alick has an interesting story,' he said, softly as if what was to come was a matter of great delicacy. 'He's a Vietnam vet. Both his parents died during his last tour of duty. That's why he can't live in the farmhouse anymore. Too many memories, I suppose.'

'Right,' Fiona said. She waited to see if the doctor would say more, but he didn't.

The nurse finished with the vial and the paperwork. She gave Lochie a drink of orange juice and helped him to sit. His short legs hung over the edge of the bed. 'There now,' she said, steadying him. 'What a brave boy you are.' She looked over to Fiona. 'Is he able to swallow tablets?'

'Not well,' Fiona said. 'Is that a problem?'

The doctor cleared his throat. 'You might want to grind the tablets and mix them with juice. The antibiotic is a little bitter.'

'Oh, I see. Well, thank you, doctor,' Fiona said, standing.

'Call me Peter.' The doctor rose and extended a hand toward her.

'Thank you, Peter.'

Life in the small town moved at its own pace. People strolled beneath the old shop awnings. Cars moved along the dome of bitumen that was the wide main street and in and out of the angled parking spaces at the kerb. Had Lochie's prognosis been dire, it would have changed nothing, Fiona knew. People would still buy their bread, go to the bank, and drink coffee at the fly-blown cafe. Trouble, she knew, was invisible and it was everywhere.

She led Lochie to the car and settled him in the back seat. He fell asleep immediately. Up ahead she could see a white sign with PHARMACY emblazoned on it and set off toward it. An old man sitting on a bench nodded to her as she passed. She was reminded of the farmer standing on the ridge with his gun resting on his hip. She wondered again whether she should be worried. Both the real estate agent and the doctor had seemed wary of him, but then she knew in her heart it was not the farmer who frightened her most. It was herself … and Richard. She needed to do better. There could be nothing for Richard to use against her.

As she was about to enter the pharmacy, Fiona was jostled and jolted. She found herself jammed against a young man with a large hiking pack on his back in the alcove leading to the entrance doors. Fiona felt the scrape of the pack on her arm as they pushed themselves free.

'Sorry,' the young man said in a strong accent. 'I'm very sorry.'

'That's okay. It was my fault,' she said. 'I wasn't concentrating.'

The young man looked at her blankly, nodded, and disappeared out of the door.

❋

'Bubble, bubble, toil and trouble', one would think watching the woman grind the tiny tablets to white dust, smaller than dust. She drops the powder in his wine. She sees his blood in it. The Body of Richard. She doesn't want to kill him, just make him sleep. Fiona stirs and waits until it glows again like old stained glass and she smiles, for she is almost gone. The smile deepens and she laughs. It's involuntary, this laugh. She is shocked. The silence from the lounge room extends. He has antenna, not fine filaments, but thick, ropey vines which sniff and grasp at the air. It has escalated. He is no longer calmed by her carefully arranged passivity. He sees Hugh as a threat now. This is why they must leave.

'Fiona, where is my wine?' He sighs a sigh strong enough to move through walls. 'I hope you haven't corked it again.'

'No.' She is quick to answer. They are mostly screw tops these days, but he doesn't know that. The world is moving on from him, all of them moving on. She smiles again.

He feels it. 'Fuck, Fiona!' he yells. This has become her name.

She must go to him now. She knows he is reluctant to move from the recliner, but if he senses her hesitance, he will, with uncanny speed, launch himself. He will come, keep coming, and he won't stop.

'Fiona!'

'I've cut a little cheese for you,' she calls to him.

'Is it Brie or Cheddar?' he asks, laying mines for her to trip.

'A little of both,' she answers.

She lifts the platter and the wine, which is clear of sediment now, and walks through to the lounge. Richard reclines, waiting for her. The children are there too, as close to the exits as the furniture will allow. She smiles at Lochie and then Hugh before she comes into his line of vision. She pushes them both from the room with the power of her mind.

'You two have homework to do, do you not?' she asks them.

'Yes,' Richard interjects. 'Go study and no headphones. You can't learn with that rubbish pumping through your skulls.' He wants them to hear, particularly Hugh.

The children melt from the room. She knows they will sit at their desks, but she also knows they will snake their earbuds up through their shirts and behind their necks into their ears, so not a hint of cord will show. She wishes Hugh oblivion in the crash and screech of his heavy metal music.

Fiona knows to approach Richard up close. She will not show her physical distaste. She sits on the arm of the chair and passes the platter and the wine to him. The outside of her upper thigh rests against his arm. He holds the platter, placing it in his lap, so she has to reach over him for the cheese.

'You are not drinking,' he says.

'No, I don't feel like it.'

'You are no fun at all, are you?' His voice has hardened.

'Okay, I'll have one with you.' She rises and goes back into the kitchen. He likes her drunk. She is less guarded, more malleable, more biddable and more likely to make a mistake.

She returns to him, so he can begin his ritual. He pretends to know wines. He makes a show of it. He lifts his glass up to the light and studies the colour. He sips and glances at her to see if she is attentive. Satisfied, he nods toward her glass. 'Wine is meant to be enjoyed, not held as a prop.'

Fiona sips. The flash of anger sours the alcohol in her mouth.

'What do you think?' he asks as if it were he who bought the wine, opened it and served it to her.

'It's velvety,' she says, willing him to drink again.

He does, only to disagree with her. 'No … no,' he says, swirling the wine in his mouth. 'I would say there's a berry aftertaste, so a little astringent. Not velvety at all.'

His eyes rest on her, waiting. She sips again, a minute droplet only.

'Hmm, I think you are right,' she agrees.

He reaches for the cheese. She sees the gold wedding ring, the hard, raised edges of it.

'Have a piece,' he says.

She must turn inward and lean over him. Her breast brushes his hand while her own reaches toward the platter. He cups her breast just enough to halt her, but not hard enough to extinguish passion. She knows this about him. He thinks she desires him. At times like this, she knows he is crazy.

He arranges his fingers to tease her nipple and she recognises her mistake. He has seen the two cheeses as a sign that she wants him. Her stomach turns as his fingers tweak and massage. He angles his lips toward her, his eyes bright with desire. She must lean in. Her buttocks slide across the leather and into his lap. His penis is beneath her now, his tongue obtrusive. She knows while she is kissing him, he is not drinking. Slowly, she draws away.

'What is it?' he asks, his voice thick.

'Would you like another wine? I know how stressed you are.'

Fiona watches as he considers this. His brow furrows.

'Okay,' he says, before swallowing the contents of his glass.

In rare moments, he can still sound like a real person. But then he is quick to add, 'Lose the knickers on the way back.'

Time slows for Fiona. She places his glass on the kitchen bench and pours the un-doctored wine. She decides she wants him to die. Her anger is a live thing, pushing through to her lungs, inflating them wide like bellows, and then collapsing them like sad balloons. Her head thrums and her scalp prickles. She can kill him. She can add the entire bottle of pills, but she will need to crush them and she doesn't have time. He will come looking.

She raises her skirt and hooks her finger on the thin fabric of her underpants. She can stay one more night. Tomorrow, she will crush all of the pills and put an end to him. Her hand trembles as she pulls the soft underwear down her legs. She picks up the full glass and walks back into the lounge room.

Richard is unconscious, his slug-like penis on display. She throws a rug in his lap and goes to the boys, first Hugh and then Lochie. Their bags are packed and ready.

Fiona was returned to the farmhouse kitchen abruptly, when the screen door was wrenched open with such force it crashed into the exterior wall of the house. The pestle clattered in the stone bowl and a puff of Lochie's antibiotic dust rose into the air.

'Mum! Mum!'

Hugh's footsteps were urgent on the wood floors. She saw his white face searching for her as he rushed into the kitchen. A chill ran through her. 'What is it?'

'The farmer shot his cow,' Hugh said.

'What?'

'I was in the veggie garden and the farmer was up on the ridge. Then all of a sudden, he dropped flat and fired at the cows under the big tree. A cow fell over.' Hugh's eyes were round with horror. 'I think it's dead.'

'I'm coming,' she said.

*

Alick stood motionless on the ridge. The rifle lay on the ground. While Fiona was crossing the membrane between the past and present, so was Alick. The tension, which never really left him, was foremost. He was back in the paddies, his sight and hearing supernaturally strained where ear drums perforated and optic nerves snapped.

He knew the steer, the moment it dropped. He considered it his lead cow, one in a long line of successive lead cows. Immediately, he mourned its loss and his part in it. The other steers, which had run at the gunshot, were returning to mill around under the tree. Over and over, they nudged the fallen steer and called to it.

Alick heard the door to the old farmhouse rattle and slam. The noise of it ricocheted through the valley like another bullet. It was the older boy. The one he'd seen running in the paddock. They would leave now, the people in the farmhouse. They would move on toward another life. The garden would disappear, camouflaged with weeds, and all would be as it was.

A bobbing object in the distance pulled at Alick's attention. A head with a crown of yellow hair appeared above the dip of the track leading from the road. Shoulder, chest, waist, hips and legs appeared, as the stranger made his way up the hill. Alick, still with a hint of sniper in his eye, could tell it was a young man and, by the hunch of his shoulders, that he carried a pack.

As the stranger drew level with the farmhouse, the screen door opened and the woman and the boy burst onto the verandah. The stranger stopped and turned to them. Alick watched as they exchanged a few words. Then he saw the young man continue up the track, through the fence and across the paddock toward him.

Alick saw the pack clearly now – full of essentials for the world traveller. Something old stirred in him.

'Hello, hello,' the young man called out.

Alick raised a hand in greeting.

'I am Sven. I am looking for work,' the young man said in heavily accented English. 'I help with your cows.'

'Right,' said Alick.

'I come from Sweden. I am working my way around your country,' Sven added. 'I sleep in tent. I camp outside.'

'Right,' said Alick again, transfixed by this unexpected event.

'So, you can give me work, yes?'

Alick's mind snapped to. 'Yes,' he said. 'Come on, lad!'

＊

She watched the young man walk away from her, down the path, back onto the track and up the hill toward the farmer. Hugh stood beside her, watching too. She saw them meet on the crest of the hill and all the while she felt things had changed so much almost nothing was the same; that this life was cut from another altogether. Fiona allowed her gaze to travel downward toward the tree. Cows milled there and while she could see little in the way of death, she sensed it. What crime had been committed that required a firing squad? She knew not enough about cows or about farming them to guess. Fiona sensed Hugh was also looking toward the tree where the cow had fallen. They were for a moment in accord, but then he said, 'I'm going back to the garden,' and she knew his anger towards her had returned even stronger than before. Perhaps he was right to be mad at her. It was she who had chosen this place.

She sat in an old wicker chair on the verandah because she knew there could be no going on about her day. She watched as the farmer and the young backpacker walked down the hill toward the tree and then back up again to disappear over the ridge.

She crept inside to check on Lochie, who was still sleeping. His temperature was beginning to fall as the antibiotic did its work. Fiona made coffee and brought it out onto the verandah to sit vigil once more. She heard the old truck before she saw it, red and rusted, cresting the ridge. It passed her on the track, the farmer in the driver's seat; the backpacker, now devoid of his pack, sitting on the wooden boards in the back next to a bale of hay. They slowed as they came abreast of her. She looked in at the farmer sitting high in the cabin. He showed her nothing but his profile.

The gate leading into the paddock was opened wide and left that way even after the truck had jostled through the mud at its entrance. Swatches of hay were thrown. The cows abandoned their fallen comrade and followed the truck back through the gate and onto the track. The procession moving past her of truck and cows was slow, funereal. She swayed with it, playing her own internal dirge.

When the haunches of the last cow had made its way over the ridge and she was left with the rising smell of live leather and animal manure, she dared herself to look back toward the tree. The steer lay neatly on its side, as if sleeping, its hide turned to her. The branches of the enormous tree hung over it and she regretted that such a thing should have happened there. She wondered whether there was blood on the ground and, if so, how much time needed to pass before all trace of it was gone.

Fiona heard the truck again. When it breached the crest of the hill, she saw it was driven by the backpacker. The farmer followed on the tractor. This time, there were no cows. There was work to be done.

The truck pulled up by the dead steer and the backpacker jumped to the ground. The farmer did likewise. They busied themselves around the steer with ropes. Another rope was thrown over a branch of the tree and it swung for a moment. The farmer tied something to it and fed the long end back to the tractor. He started the engine and the tractor jolted forward. Fiona heard the creaking of the ropes as they took the strain. The dead steer rose in the air and began to twirl. Her phone shrilled. It peeled out across the valley and she imagined across the slope to the big tree. She scrambled for it on the floor beside her chair and brought it to her ear while the cow continued to sway in the air.

'Hello,' she said.

'Hello, is that Fiona Lees?'

'Yes,' she said, watching the backpacker walk to the truck and start the engine.

'It's Michael Green from Fair Work Nation.'

'Yes, yes,' Fiona replied, watching as the tray of the truck backed under the swinging cow and the tractor slowly reversed to lower the cow down onto it.

'Fiona?'

'Yes. Oh, I'm sorry, Michael,' she said.

'Are you okay?'

'Everything is fine,' she said.

'Right then. I have an interview date for you. Renee Rodgers, one of our best advocates, will be in the Brisbane office this Tuesday.'

'Tuesday is fine with me,' she said.

'What about eleven o'clock?' Michael Green asked.

The farmer, the backpacker, and the cow passed by her on the track. The truck hit a bump and the cow's head lolled toward her. In the centre of its forehead was a neat bullet hole.

'Eleven sounds fine.'

A VET CALLED HARRY

Daisy lowed deep from within her chest cavity and Alick felt the vibrations of it through her hide. He placed the bucket beneath her hindquarters and the milking stool behind him and she settled somewhat. He planted his own feet and stretched tall in preparation, so he might huddle more effectively. The horizon caught his eye and he looked out toward the mountains in the east where the day was brewing. There would be no rain today. He didn't expect good rain for months now, had no right to since summer had ended. Spring would need to treat them right or the fires would come through. He hawked some phlegm in the back of his throat and spat. It felt good to think of simple things, like rain or the lack of it.

From where Alick stood, he could not see the tree beyond the ridge, but it came to him again as it had done over the last few days. He saw the light as it was then, furred around the edges by the humidity and a deep, secretive green under the roof of leaves. He felt the wind too, slight, imperceptible to most, but not to him. The shot rang out again, just as it had, and Alick slumped onto the milking stool and nestled into Daisy's flank. His hands shook as he rolled her teats between his thumbs and forefingers. Daisy took a billowing kick out to the side, but tucked in as he was, she could not reach him. He brought the milk down out of her udder and it splashed in the bucket, the steam rising, and in his mind Alick saw the cow swinging from the tree, dangling there like a dead Marine. Tomorrow, he would need to collect the meat from Sweeney's.

Daisy sent out a hoof again and connected with Alick's tailbone. 'For fuck's sake!' Alick roared, teetering on the stool and grabbing the bucket to save the milk. Daisy turned her head and rolled an eye at him, her ears flattened to back of her head and her breath blasting through her round nostrils. 'You stop that, old cow, or I'll sell you on,' he said to her rolling eye. 'You behave yourself, darling.'

Alick took her teats between his fingers again and bent to his task. Pain blossomed in his lower back as he positioned himself again. He'd have a bruise, he thought, be sore for a few days, but then that's what happens when a mind is not on the job.

With his head resting hidden against Daisy's flank, Alick felt the cow's tension build again in her muscles. 'What's up?' he asked, stopping his milking and running a hand up over her udder. It was hot to the touch and Daisy made to kick him again. Alick located a lump high up and to the rear of the udder. 'Bloody hell, old pet,' he said. 'It's mastitis! We'll need to drain you good and proper, which neither of us are going to like, and call Harry in.'

❋

Fiona's heels echoed over the scuffed wooden floor as she approached the front desk at Fair Work Nation. 'Fiona Lees to see Renee Rodgers,' she told the receptionist.

'Yes, of course. Just take a seat and I'll let her know you've arrived,' the woman replied.

Fiona sat on a sagging sofa in the small visitors' alcove. Across from her were two chairs with burst, brown vinyl upholstery and on the wall a large print of a sinking ship hung lopsidedly. Her phone trilled in her handbag and she fished it out. Her thumb was poised to answer when she saw it was Richard. She scrabbled for the off button to silence it and the phone fell and skittered across the floor coming to rest under the vinyl chair. The receptionist looked up as the phone rang and rang. Fiona nodded to her and dove for it, this time connecting with the off button. She resumed her seat, wiping dust and grit from her trousers. She took deep breaths to calm herself, but it was already too late. A switch had been tripped and Richard stood before her, spitting his anger at her, his hand around the back of her neck anchoring her in front of him.

'Ms Lees! Fiona!'

Richard faded. The receptionist was crossing the floor between them, her concern ready. Fiona did not want it and she would not accept it. She gathered her bag in her clammy hands.

'Are you all right?' the receptionist asked her.

'I'm quite all right,' she said.

'But you're shaking,' the receptionist said.

'Really, I'm fine.' Fiona clasped her hands around her bag to still them.

The receptionist stepped back. 'Okay, then. Mr Green and Ms Rodgers will see you now.'

Fiona followed her past the reception desk, down a dull corridor with more prints of sinking ships, and into a room at the hall's end.

A man stepped toward her with his hand outstretched. 'Hello Fiona, I'm Michael Green. We spoke on the phone,' he said, shaking her hand and smiling. 'Just thought I'd drop in and put a face to the voice, so to speak.'

'It's nice to meet you, Michael.' Fiona felt her pulse slow.

A woman rose from her chair and introduced herself as Renee Rodgers. They stood for an instant, poised, a diorama of the mid-level business meeting.

Michael Green was the first to move. 'Well, I'll get on, shall I? It was nice to meet you, Fiona.' He smiled, nodded to them both and left the room.

'Please sit,' Renee Rodgers said.

Fiona made herself comfortable and arranged her pen, notebook and digital recorder on the desk before her. There was only the hint of a tremor in her fingertips. Once set, she addressed the advocate. 'Thank you for agreeing to talk with me,' she said. 'As Michael has probably told you, I am a journalist with *In Business* and I'm working on a feature about workplace bullying. We are hoping you will be able to give us some insight into the issue.'

'Of course.' Renee Rodgers cupped one hand in the other and placed them on the table in front of her, her body leaning in. 'What would you like to know? I'm a trained psychologist as well, if that helps?'

'It does. Perhaps we could start there, then,' Fiona said. 'In my research, there is a lot about bullying amongst children and adolescents, but not much when it comes to adults. I'm wondering if you can speculate as to why?'

Renee Rodgers was already nodding in response. 'I think there are a lot of misconceptions in this area. It's getting better. I mean, there are some more studies coming out and there are some policies in place to recognise bullying in the workplace, but there is still a long way to go.'

'Why do you think that is, Ms Rodgers?'

The advocate smiled broadly at Fiona. 'Oh, please call me Renee and I'll call you Fiona, if I may?'

'Of course.'

'You know, one tends to think adults would be beyond all this; neither fragile enough to be a victim or aggressive enough to be a bully. There is often the belief that adults would recognise and operate within the bounds of fair play, but, sadly, it's not true.'

It wasn't often that a source was both thoughtful and literate. Fiona could already feel the bones of a good story emerging. 'So, would it be true to say a child bully becomes an adult bully?'

'Not always. Sometimes a child simply grows out of it. Some insight is gained as the person moves into adulthood. Interestingly enough, these people can become quite protective and supportive of adult victims.' Renee rocked her head to one side, as if what she learned still surprised her. Then she shook that thought away and continued on. 'What is even more interesting is that childhood victims of bullying have a chance of growing into an adult bully.'

Fiona raised an eyebrow. 'Settling old scores, do you think?'

'We don't really know and it's dangerous to speculate. That's where more studies would come in handy.'

Fiona nodded. 'So, may I ask you what you do in your role as advocate?'

'Okay, Fair Work Nation works as a third party in situations where bullying has been reported in the workplace, but little has been done to address it.'

'Does that happen often?' Fiona asked.

'Oh yes. If you go back to the belief that bullying shouldn't happen in the adult world, you can see, even with the new anti-bullying legislation, how workplaces can minimise the problem or dismiss it altogether.'

'In what ways do they do that?'

'Well, often it is the victim who is blamed.'

'Really?'

'Yes, I know. It's pretty rough when you have had the courage to report the bullying in the first place, but it's all too common. Victims can be characterised as weak and overly sensitive. The bullying can be put down to a managerial style.'

'So, victims are ignored?'

'They can be, yes, and the bullying can continue unchecked. There are cases where the workplace in question has been exposed as a hot-bed for bullying.'

'Can you give me an example of this?'

'Certainly. I'll give you a copy of Conway vs Shelton. It's famous for all the wrong reasons.' Renee opened a drawer beside her desk and took out a thick document and placed it in front of Fiona. 'The behaviour of the respondent was considered sufficient for the court to deem it endemic within the company,' she said, indicating the court transcript.

'So, let me get this right,' Fiona said. 'Had Conway's lawyers not been able to show that the bullying was permissible within Shelton Industries, the case would have been thrown out?'

'Yes, that's exactly it. Shelton vs Conway was the first time bullying became a serious issue for business and often the bigger the business, the bigger the issue,' Renee said.

'How big is it exactly?' Fiona asked.

'It's big. In dollar terms, we suspect it can cost companies millions,' Renee said.

'You suspect?' Fiona prompted.

'Well, yes. We can't know. Except for Conway vs Shelton where Shelton was directed to pay $2 million in damages, everyone else settles and confidentiality agreements are signed.' Renee raised her arms from the table and shrugged. 'We simply can't know, but we think $2 million is chicken feed now.'

Fiona sat for a while, allowing Renee Rodger's words to sink in. 'Okay. So, putting aside the settlements and the confidentiality clauses, is there anyone you have worked with I can talk to?' Fiona asked.

'Not really. You see, that's the problem. These companies pay damages, yes, but they don't see it as that. They see it as a way to keep the story out of the press and stop it from going any further,' Renee said. 'Basically, it's hush money.'

'Right. Do you think the confidentiality clauses allow companies to perpetuate bullying?' Fiona asked.

'Well, that's the question, isn't it? I don't know that companies would like to be paying out large sums to keep workplace bullies on board, but it could make room for them to get creative in how they frame bullying in the first place,' Renee said.

'I'm sorry, Renee. I don't understand,' Fiona said.

'That's okay. This stuff isn't talked about at all. That's the problem. If people don't know what constitutes bullying, except in extreme cases, like Shelton vs Conway, companies will define it and lots of unacceptable behaviour falls through the cracks. It's like sexual harassment was back in the day and arguably still is. What's okay and what's not, can be a fine line, but someone needs to draw it. It can't remain a matter of opinion,' Renee said.

'Okay,' Fiona said, taking a big breath.

Renee leaned across the desk and said firmly, 'If you and your magazine reinforce correct definitions of it, that would help.'

Fiona nodded. 'Of course. Who else can I talk to, Renee?'

Renee opened her diary and ran a finger down the page and then looked up. 'Give Gordie Watts a ring. He's an expert on workplace culture. He'll be able to give you an idea of how these toxic workplaces develop. He's great. He's done some studies, which may give some real-world examples.'

The name was familiar to Fiona. She flipped through her notebook and there it was. She looked up at Renee. 'He also does stuff on sexual harassment, doesn't he?'

Renee said, 'Yes, I think he does. How do you know him?'

'Well, I don't, but he's speaking at an organisational psychology conference I'll be attending next month.'

'It's a small world, isn't it?' Renee said.

'Yes, it is,' Fiona agreed.

It didn't matter how long she had been a feature writer, the fizz of excitement over the beginnings of a good story hadn't left her. It began in her belly and spread to the tips of her fingers. Was it too early to ring Steph with the good news? Even with editors she knew well, she was wary to talk a story up. Too much could happen to torpedo it, but the urge was strong. When her mobile phone rang, she answered it, almost hoping it was Steph, and then fearing it was Richard. 'Hello?'

'Is that Fiona Lees?' The voice was unfamiliar.

'Yes, speaking,' Fiona said, relief flooding in.

'It's Dr Edgerton – Peter Edgerton. I have the results back from your son's blood tests.'

'Oh yes?'

'It was Australian Spotted Fever, as we thought,' the doctor said. 'The antibiotics should have cleared it right up. He is well now, isn't he?'

'Yes, Lochie is fine. Thank you, doctor.'

A small pause descended between them. Fiona changed lanes, preparing to take the next exit off the motorway. 'Was there anything else, doctor?'

'Please, call me Peter,' the doctor said.

'Okay.'

The doctor cleared his throat. 'There was something else. We are celebrating the 150-year anniversary of our local hall next weekend and I was wondering if you would like to go? It would be a way of meeting some of the locals.'

'An anniversary?'

'Yes. Our little community is quite an old one, in relative terms, of course.'

'Really?' Fiona smiled to herself when she realised the doctor was nervous. 'I suppose I could come,' she said. This is what people did, after all.

*

They waited by the home paddock – the farmer, the young man, and the dairy cow. Alick had the milking stool out. He rested one of his feet on it and braced his elbows over his raised knee to take the pressure off his back. The boy leaned nearby on the wooden fence bordering the house paddock, one leg cocked behind him on the lowest rail. Alick and Sven were waiting for Harry, the vet.

Alick lifted his foot off the stool and placed it on the ground to stretch his back. The hoof-sized ache radiated up his spine to his shoulder blades and down his leg. He placed the other foot on the stool, elbows once again on his knee. All the time he was aware of the boy. There were not many who could stand without fidgeting and shuffling about. He was also a handy lad, a good boy in a crisis. He neither overplayed or underplayed the situation, but just got in and did what needed to be done.

Alick heard Harry's big off-road vehicle. A plume of dust from the track floated to them from over the ridge and Daisy let out one of her deep bone-twitching lows. Alick changed feet again as Harry came into view.

The vet killed the engine and dropped to the ground.

'Sorry to be late, Alick. Old Robsen out on Gap Road let his pony into the chook feed again. Blew up like a piñata, she did. Had to let the gas out.' Harry spoke as he crossed the distance between the van and Alick. It was then that he noticed the young backpacker.

'So, this is the young chap I've heard about. Good to see. Good to see.' The vet shook Sven's hand. 'Haven't I been telling you to get some help around here?'

Alick refused to acknowledge this one way or another.

'Hmm,' said Harry, still evaluating Sven. 'He seems okay. Handy, I would say.' Then without pause, Harry strode off toward the home paddock, snapping on his surgical gloves.

'He doesn't speak much English, though,' Alick called after him.

'Just as well. Neither do you,' Harry said, ducking through the fence and sidling up to Daisy. His hands palpated the udder and Daisy took exception with a billowing kick out to the side. Harry sidled in too close for the hoof and Daisy was thwarted.

'Hey, young man,' he called, waving an arm toward Sven. 'Come in here and steady her, will you? No lady likes her tits groped without an invitation.'

Alick watched as Harry positioned the young backpacker facing Daisy with one hand gripping either side of her halter.

'Keep her head straight, mate,' Harry yelled. 'If she can't see me, she can't kick me.'

The young man and the cow stared at each other, while Harry examined Daisy's udder. Quiet fell over them and the world seemed to slow to a resting pace. A kookaburra called from the creek, rain's false prophet. Alick swapped legs again and the pain eased in his back.

Snap! Snap! Harry stepped away from Daisy's rear, removing his gloves.

'He's a good lad,' Harry said, cocking his head toward Sven. 'You can tell a lot about a chap by how he is with animals.'

'Is that right?' Alick said.

'Except for you, old man,' Harry said, handing over the antibiotic paste for Alick. 'You're the exception to my rule.' Harry slapped Alick on the back.

Alick winced.

'What's up with you?' the vet asked.

'Just a bit of a twinge in the old back,' Alick said. 'It will settle down.'

Harry stopped. 'Do you want me to take a look? People and animals, not that different, you know.'

'I'm different,' said Alick.

Harry smiled. 'That you are, Alick. That you are.'

In minutes, Harry was gone, and the boy and the cow were his only company. Alick stood tall and picked up the stool. The boy climbed through the rails of the fence, nodded to Alick, and set off toward the ridge where he'd made camp.

'Do you want lunch?' Alick called.

The boy stopped.

'Food, you know?' Alick mimed putting food in his mouth and chewing.

Sven nodded. 'Yes. Food. Thank you.'

✳

Lunch was comprised of canned corn, beetroot, pickles and corned meat laid out in resealable plastic containers. The young man ate steadily, as was his habit.

'You could have a shelf in the fridge in the shed, if you like,' the old farmer said. 'I'll show you what I mean later.'

'Thank you,' the young man replied.

Alick rose and left the table. There was chinking of china and the sigh of an electric kettle, but Sven focussed on the plate in front of him. Only when he had finished the last mouthful, did he notice his surroundings.

Everything – floors, bench-tops, table and chairs – were laminated; as processed as the food. But this was not the most surprising thing. Cardboard boxes lined every wall, from the floor to the ceiling, as far as the eye could see. The young man could tell that the boxes had been there for a long time. The base of each box had collapsed into the top of the one beneath, until it was difficult to figure out where one box began, and another ended.

Alick returned from the kitchen with tea and Anzac biscuits. The young man watched the farmer as he ate his biscuit and drank his tea. He saw how he twisted in his chair to ease his back and how his calloused hands would tremble and then grow still again.

BUTCHERED

The thought was present when Fiona awoke. It flapped about like a landed fish. She rolled over and squinted out of the window and into the glare of the new day. Her decision to go out with the doctor was absurd. What made her think she could smile and nod and make conversation? She had done so once, but it was different now.

Crows cawed in the background as she swung her legs over the edge of the bed. She felt a chill across her shoulders and was driven to an old wooden wardrobe for a jumper. When she entered the kitchen, Hugh was sitting at the table in front of his laptop. 'Shouldn't you be getting ready for school?' she asked him.

He frowned and shook his head. 'It's a pupil-free day, Mum. I told you. Lochie has the day off too.'

'What? Both of you?'

'Yes, it's the strike, remember?'

No, she did not remember. She stood over the sink filling the kettle with water for tea. She received the school's emails, but no longer read them. Through the window, the crows were fanning out across the sky. She watched as they came back together again and settled in the big old tree in the paddock, noisy as bats. Her mind travelled back to the dead cow day, the carcass spinning in the air.

'Mum?'

'Yes?'

'I was thinking we could go into town and buy some seeds for the garden. And maybe a hose?'

'Yes, that's a good idea.' They had done nothing as a family since her mother's theatre production. Pulling them together had been beyond her. 'I have some work to do this morning, but we could go later,' Fiona said, stepping away from the window.

'Bullying is detrimental to workplace culture as a whole, Fiona. One bully can destroy a lot of good feeling. View it as an infection of sorts.'

Fiona could already tell Gordon Watts was a seasoned media performer. Almost every utterance was quotable. 'How do you mean?' she asked, resting the phone in the crook of her neck, so she could make rapid notes.

'Whether management is the problem, or they are unaware of it, unbridled bullying can turn a workplace from a collection of vibrant, creative and collaborative workers into individuals who are distrustful, disgruntled, often absent from work and, when present, largely unproductive. Lines of communication break down and teamwork can become next to impossible. So, I would have to say, prevention is better than cure.'

'Are you saying a workplace can be designed where bullying can't occur?'

'Nothing is 100% foolproof, but the place to start is with a clearly thought-out interpersonal philosophy – a code of conduct, if you like. Write what you expect in terms of behaviour and be precise. The mistake a lot of managing directors make is to assume good behaviour as a default. I advise against this.'

'Okay, how should this document be used?'

'It is foundational. It drives the kinds of people who are hired in the first place. It clearly and publicly indicates the kinds of behaviours which are unacceptable. It provides fair warning, if you like.'

'I see.' Just like the mission statements of the nineties, Fiona thought. Written and soon forgotten.

'I know what you are thinking. They can't be like the old mission statement idea either.'

Fiona smiled. Gordon Watts certainly had all his bases covered.

'Writing a code of conduct and ignoring it would be worse than not having one at all. The lack of sincerity would create the perfect culture to foster rather than discourage bullying.'

'So, it's all about sincerity?'

'Sure. You have to mean it. There can't be any cracks. Bullies love a loophole.'

Once again, Watts had provided the perfect quote. Fiona wrote it down. 'Can we go back to the hiring of staff? How does one weed out potential bullies?'

'I grant you, it's difficult. Often bullies will attempt to steer their own job interview. They can be quick to criticise previous workplaces. Their language can be geared to what a company can do for them rather than how they can add value. These are a few of the tells, but some bullies can be very charming when they want something, such as a job, but are diabolical when they perceive they are in a position of power.'

'Renee mentioned childhood victims of bullying can become adult bullies. What do you think?'

'I suppose that is very possibly true. A victim would have a fairly ingrained, but skewed perception of power. Everyone is either a victim or a bully, for example. However, while it may be Renee's job to understand the bully, it is mine to protect workplaces from them, if you see what I mean?'

'I do.' Fiona couldn't help but like Watts. His mission was clear.

'In a workplace where bullying is not tolerated, a person must cease the behaviour or find work elsewhere.'

'Is it that simple?' Fiona asked.

'Well, there may be a period where they belittle whatever doesn't enable them to bully. We saw this at the turn of this century as organisational psychology really started to gain a foothold and highlighted a healthy workplace culture. There were a lot of naysayers. We've moved on a bit from there, but not as much as you might think. While there are laws written into workplace health and safety legislation to accommodate an employer's duty of care to the psychological health of a worker, a lot of bullying goes unreported. I'm sure Renee mentioned this.'

'Yes, she did. Victims are already too vulnerable.'

'Exactly.'

'Well, thank you, Gordon. You have been very helpful, and I don't want to take up any more of your time.'

'It's been a pleasure, Fiona. Actually, I'll be up your way in a few weeks, I think. A conference.'

'I know. I was going to interview you then about your work on gender in the workplace for another story.'

'Really?'

'Yup.'

'Well, I will look forward to it.'

'Me too.'

*

'Sven. Svennnn.' There was a lot of lip and teeth and tongue involved. It sounded odd. Awkward to pronounce. Sven.

Alick stepped gingerly out of the truck in front of Sweeney's Butchers. He left the keys in the ignition and slammed the door because that was what was needed to keep it closed.

'Hello, Alick. I hear you have a nice family in the old farmhouse.'

'What?' Alick spun around and found the local doctor standing on the kerb smiling pleasantly.

'The woman renting the old farmhouse?'

Alick frowned. 'So, what's it to you?'

The doctor shook his head and stepped away with his arms raised, as if to fend Alick off. 'I was being polite, just making conversation.'

The gesture irritated Alick. Did he honestly think a near 80-year-old would take a pot-shot at him? 'Well, I'm not polite and I don't make conversation.'

'I can see that,' the doctor said, moving away.

Alick felled the doctor with a mental punch to the bridge of the nose, grimaced and walked into Sweeney's.

Art stood behind the counter with his knives strapped on, a master of illegal butchery. 'Hey Alick! Sorry I wasn't here when you brought the beast in. I was in the city at the bloody accountant's.' Art opened the swing door to the side of the counter and came through. He thrust a three-fingered hand at Alick and Alick shook it feeling uneasy about it, as he always did. He wondered why Art didn't extend the other hand. People would understand it with the three fingers and all.

'Throw your keys to young Daryl, over there. He can bring your truck around back,' Art said.

The young apprentice came through the swinging door and stood by, awaiting Alick's keys.

'The keys are in the truck, son,' Alick said. 'The rusted thing at the kerb.'

The boy nodded and Alick followed Art, with his knives glittering, through the butchery to the back refrigerator beside a loading bay.

'I hear you have a young off-sider now. The boys told me he was some kind of foreigner,' Art said on the way.

'Swedish,' Alick said.

'Good lad, they said. Helpful. Strong and all that.' Art stopped and nodded toward young Daryl – who was putting his shoulder to the door of Alick's truck to escape it – and Ben, his own son, and Frankie, his nephew. 'Don't know what I would do without these young'uns now.'

Alick nodded. In the past, the value of a young off-sider would not have crossed his mind.

As Daryl, Ben and Frankie carried the cardboard boxes from the freezer to the tray of Alick's truck, Alick wondered at what point he had become old to other people. Certainly, it was before he felt it or knew it himself. Art was talking again. 'Ben told me it was one hell of a shot, Alick. Not many can say they can kill a beast so clean ... and from a distance too, or so it looked?' Art said. 'Best marksman in the district is old Alick, I told them. Sniped those Viet Cong for the Army, I said.'

Alick said nothing. Those who hadn't gone talked. Those who went stayed silent. That was the way of it.

*

The sky was a perfect blue and the paddocks a perfect green. The mountains, which fringed the valley, hung against the sky and were a dusky purple. Even the cows and horses they passed appeared artfully arranged, black and white and rich browns like cut-outs against the green, green grass. Lochie was chattering about the boys at school and one girl in particular, Janine, but Fiona had ceased listening. She understood this place she had escaped to was beautiful. It didn't have to be. She'd had no expectation of it.

'Don't be stupid,' Hugh said to Lochie.

'I'm not stupid,' Lochie replied.

'Girls don't like the fat kid,' Hugh said.

Fiona snapped to attention. Hugh's words were bad enough, but it was his tone which sent shivers through her. 'Stop it, Hugh. Lochie is just fine as he is,' she said. She looked in the rear-vision mirror at her oldest son and she saw him roll his eyes at her.

'No, you stop it, Mum. Lochie is not going to get it if you keep sugar-coating everything for him,' Hugh snapped, as they entered the small main street.

'What is Lochie supposed to get exactly, Hugh?' Fiona asked and immediately regretted it.

Hugh's gaze slid to meet her own in the mirror. 'He needs to know he's a loser, so he can do something about it.'

'I am not,' yelled Lochie.

Fiona could hear the beginnings of tears in his voice.

'You're the loser, Hugh!' he shouted.

Hugh shook his head as they pulled into a park outside the produce store. 'You really are stupid,' Hugh said to Lochie, opening the door and stepping out of the car. 'Dead stupid,' he said, before slamming the car door and striding off into the store.

'Lochie, don't listen to him,' Fiona said, when he slumped in the car seat. 'Come on, why don't we go and get us some seeds for the garden.' Fiona opened her door, but when she turned back to check on Lochie he had not moved. She sat still with him, staring out through the windscreen.

'Mum?'

Fiona turned to face him.

'Everything's different now,' he said.

'Yes, it is.'

'Do you think it will get back to how it was?' Lochie asked.

Fiona felt her heart swell into her throat.

'I don't mean how it was with Dad. I don't mean that,' Lochie said. 'I mean, when does it get better?'

It was a question she also wanted an answer to. 'I don't know, Lochie. I think things change all the time and we can't really fight that, but maybe if we did some of the things we used to do ... we'd feel better?' Was that what she was doing in going out with the doctor?

Lochie looked down at his lap. 'There's Hugh's birthday, next week.' He looked up at her. 'We could have a party, maybe? Ask Grandma and Grandpa and Aunty Julia and Uncle Graham. We could show them the garden.'

Fiona smiled at him. 'You are a good boy, you know. You want to throw a party for your brother even though he's mean to you.'

'I want us to have fun,' Lochie said. 'He's nicer when he's having fun. Everyone is nicer when they are having fun.'

Not everybody, she thought. 'Okay, we'll throw a party. What do you think Hugh might like for his birthday?'

'I don't know,' Lochie said. 'We need to think about it.'

'Alright, but right now let's go and buy some seeds.'

Lochie nodded. He climbed out of the car and disappeared into the produce store. Fiona wished it were that easy. Still, they needed to try.

A grey-haired man with an impressive paunch came out from behind the front counter when Fiona entered the store. 'Do you need some help, love?'

'Yes, could you direct me to the seed aisle, please? My sons and I are putting in a vegetable garden.'

'I saw your boys. They are back there,' he said, indicating Lochie and Hugh's position with a jerk of his head. 'See that wheelbarrow up there on the stand?'

Fiona nodded. It looked precarious.

'Well, the seeds are just behind there,' he said.

'Thanks.'

Fiona found Hugh with a bunch of seed packets in his hand and, in the rickety shopping trolley beside him, there were seedling trays, a sprinkler and two bags of seed-raising mix. 'How are you going?' she asked him.

'Well, I think I've got most of the seeds,' he said. 'I've stuck with the winter ones, you know. Onions, spinach, broad beans, peas.'

'Right,' Fiona said, but nothing was right. She stared at Hugh.

'What?' His tone was insolent.

'What did Lochie ever do to you?' It came out before she had a chance to pull it back in. 'What makes you like this?'

Hugh shrugged. 'Like what?'

A lump grew in Fiona's throat. 'I know it's been difficult lately. I know that, but can't you just –'

Hugh laughed. 'Can't I just what? Make things easy? Do what you say? Do what Dad says?' His face screwed shut. 'No, I can't,' he said, pushing past her and running down the aisle.

'Hugh!' she called after him, but he was already gone.

Fiona weaved her way around islands of toolboxes, buckets and strange, dust-covered light-fittings looking for Lochie. She navigated a small wooden ramp, which took her over a trench and out into the yard at the back. Lochie stood in front of a cage of chickens. He was so intent on watching the birds scratch and peck at the grain in the bottom of the cage he didn't notice her approach. It was only when she stood very close to him that he realised she was there.

'I think I know what Hugh might like for his birthday,' he whispered.

'Things are a bit difficult right now, Lochie,' Fiona said, 'I think it's a good idea, but we might have to postpone the chickens.'

'But why?' This came out in a long, thin cry.

'I don't think Hugh wants anything right now. I don't think he wants a party either,' she said, leaning closer to Lochie.

Lochie shook his head. 'He does. He just won't say he does.'

Fiona watched Hugh plant the vegetable seeds from the kitchen window. The air inside the car on the journey home had prickled with unsaid things. As soon as she pulled the car to a stop outside the farmhouse, Hugh disappeared into the garden. Even Lochie had distanced himself, shutting himself away with his video games. What should have been a day they could spend as a family had left them as far from each other as it was possible to be. Perhaps Lochie was right. A party might be the answer.

Fiona was musing on this, when she heard knocking on the door and then a voice. 'Hello! My name is Sven!'

Fiona turned away from the window. As she walked down the hall, she could see the young backpacker through the screen door. In his hands he held a cardboard box.

'Hello,' she said, opening the door for him to step through.

'I'm Fiona,' she said, offering her hand and then withdrawing it because of the box.

He nodded to her in place of the handshake.

'Nice to meet you, Sven. What do you have there?'

'Meat,' he said. He cocked his head toward the farmer's house. 'From Alick.'

'Oh?'

'The cow, you know.'

Fiona caught on. 'Oh, the cow. Right. Come in.'

She ushered him through the sitting room into the kitchen. Sven placed the sagging box on the table.

'Would you like a drink, Sven? A glass of water, maybe?' she asked taking a pitcher of water from the refrigerator.

'No, no. I work for Alick now. I work now,' he said.

'Okay then, but thank you for bringing the meat,' Fiona said.

Sven nodded again. He left immediately, walking back through the house and down the front stairs. Fiona watched him go. Only when she heard the creaking of the hinges on the front gate did she undo the flaps of the cardboard box and look inside.

✳

As the young man walked away from the old farmhouse, he held an image of the woman in his head and he studied it. He placed her in the catalogue in his mind of people he had met. He already knew her type. She came from that world of backyard swimming pools and antique dining tables where people sat gracefully eating their meals and no one was shooting up in the bathtub.

A DALLIANCE WITH THE DOCTOR

'It will be nice to spend time with Grandma and Grandpa, don't you think?' Fiona said, as she drove Hugh and Lochie to her parents' house.

Lochie nodded and wriggled around in the passenger seat to face her. 'It'll be great! Gran said we could go to see Egyptian mummies at the museum tomorrow.'

'Right. That should be fun!' Fiona was missing him already.

Hugh remained silent in the back seat. He hadn't spoken to her in days. She felt the longer this went on, the further away from each other they would become. Perhaps this was what happened to other families? The gaps became unbridgeable.

As she parked the car in her parents' driveway, she imagined herself ringing the doctor to cancel their evening and having it out with Hugh. She could step in before it was too late. Her stomach turned at the thought of it. She wasn't ready.

Lochie rushed past his grandparents into the house. 'He has been looking forward to this,' Fiona said, as she kissed her mother on the cheek. 'He's very excited about the museum.'

'What about Hugh?' Stuart asked, as his oldest grandchild sloped toward them with his backpack trailing from one hand.

'He's sixteen, Dad. Everything is boring.'

'Hmm,' Stuart said, stepping aside as Hugh continued into the house. 'Are you sure that's all it is?'

Guilt washed over her. Fiona glanced at her father, but he turned as Hugh brushed by them and she couldn't see his face.

'Are you off to some kind of networking event?' Gwendolyn asked.

'Yes, Mum. I'm wanting to pick up work for a few more magazines.' Fiona replied, relieved at the change in topic.

'Aren't the boys and the work you already have enough? We worry about you way out there with all the things you have to do,' Gwendolyn said.

Just like that, her relief was extinguished. 'Well don't, Mum. I like my job and the boys are older now.'

Fiona has three dresses which she alternates for social occasions. Richard says he likes women to look like women. He says this often as if her gender is in question. One dress has thin straps which cross at the back and leave her shoulders bare. She wears this one when her injuries lie elsewhere. She hides them as much as Richard does and she doesn't know why. Perhaps there is something wrong inside her head.

Richard stands beside her in front of the mirrored wardrobe doors. He looks at her and then at himself. He wears chinos and a cool, linen shirt with two buttons open at the top in a manner he thinks sophisticated. Fiona has no opinion on this. She only cares that he will be unconscious soon, once she has the pills.

Fiona saw the dress or as much of it as she could in the small bathroom mirror. Habit had dressed her in it. An unwillingness to decide her own level of comfort had driven her to pull it over her head and arrange the crossed straps over her shoulder blades. She tore off the dress and threw it on the floor in a corner and picked out a pair of jeans, a shirt and a woollen sweater she'd grown fond of since the nights had cooled.

*

Sven was loading bales of hay onto a trailer when the vet drew up beside the shed. The young man shaded his eyes against the lowering sun and watched as Harry removed a carton of beer from the back seat.

'Come on, lad,' he called, motioning Sven forward. 'It's the end of the week and there's drinking to do. Where's the old man?'

By the way Alick hesitated in the doorway of his house, Sven knew Friday afternoon drinks weren't a regular thing. Harry slowed as Alick led them down the hall to the kitchen. He paused just long enough to take in the stacked cardboard boxes lining the walls, but he said nothing. Sven wondered why. In the kitchen, Harry took it upon himself to open the carton and hand out the beers. He held a can in his hand and cocked his head toward Sven. 'What do you think, Alick? Do you think the lad is old enough for ale?'

'The boy works hard. That makes him old enough,' Alick said.

Harry opened his eyes wide. 'Well, I never,' he said, slapping his knees with both hands. 'Do you know what that means, Sven, my lad?'

Sven did not.

'No, I doubt that you do.' The vet paused for effect and Alick grumbled under his breath. 'It means he likes you and … he doesn't like anybody.'

Alick grimaced, his face looking to the boy like corrugated iron. 'I don't like vets, lad. They are nosy bastards.'

Harry grinned and winked at Sven.

A silence fell over the trio as they swallowed their beer. The old man remained in no-man's land standing by the refrigerator with Sven and Harry seated at the kitchen table.

Alick cleared this throat. 'How about I cook up some steaks?'

'From one of yours?' Harry asked.

Alick's gaze slid toward Sven and rested on him. His eyes were icy blue. 'Yup,' he said to Harry, but still focussed on Sven.

'So, you've sent a beast to the abattoir?' Harry asked.

Alick jerked his chin downward in a quick nod and turned away to open the fridge freezer.

Harry put his hands to his round belly and rubbed it. 'You are in for a treat, lad. There is nothing so good as one of the old man's steaks!'

With the meat on a plate, they moved outside to a BBQ by the back door. The three of them stood around the grill, as men did, tipping beer down their throats while the steaks cooked. Harry and Alick talked of cows and meat prices and weather and Sven leant against the warm bricks of the wood-fired BBQ and listened. The old man's lie lay between them now, alongside his own.

＊

The man standing under the porch light was a stranger to her. Fiona squinted out at him, trying to place him in his surgery on the day they had met, but failed. It was as if nothing of the doctor had penetrated her worry over Lochie's illness.

Peter was shorter, quite different from the vague shape she had imagined. He was fleshier too. Pale and doughy in the cheeks. His hair was still damp and slicked backwards from a high forehead. Surely, she would have remembered such things. From the neck up, he had the look of a nineteenth century bank manager. He was younger too than she had imagined. Younger than herself, perhaps.

'I won't be a moment,' she said. She left him at the door and walked down the hall to collect her handbag and phone. How odd, she was thinking. How very odd.

'How was your week?' Peter asked her once they had settled into the front seats of his smart four-wheel drive.

'Fine,' she said. 'Very good,' she added because 'fine' didn't seem enough. 'How was yours?'

'It's an ageing population, you know, and a large district, so it's busy. Then there's the wear and tear farming takes on the body,' he said, his voice now familiar and as strangely calming as it had been in the surgery. 'Sooner or later, they pay. Mostly later,' he said.

Fiona nodded. 'What kinds of problems are we talking about?' The doctor could easily have been another interviewee.

'Lots of back problems, knee problems and a fair bit of skin cancer. It can be pretty harsh in the summer months.'

'I remember,' she agreed. 'It was summer when we moved here.'

The doctor looked across at her. 'Is it only you and your son, Lochie?'

She knew what he was asking her, but she would not answer him. 'I have another son, Hugh,' she said instead.

'Right,' Peter replied.

The hall was like nothing she had seen before. It was completely lined with varnished wooden boards. The floors, the walls, and the ceiling. Bare light bulbs hung on long black insulated wires, so the very apex of the ceiling receded into the gloom. The bulbs swung in lazy arcs each time a breeze snuck through the entrance door.

'Come,' the doctor said, taking her elbow. 'I'll introduce you to some people.'

A middle-aged woman with many bangles jingling on her wrists was the first to separate from the crowd.

'I'm Ivy,' she said, offering her hand in greeting.

'This is Fiona,' Peter said. 'She has moved into the old farmhouse.'

Ivy raised an eyebrow at Peter. 'Alick's old farmhouse you mean?'

Peter nodded.

'Well, how is he then? We don't see him much in town these days.'

'I don't see him much either,' Fiona replied. 'He keeps to himself.'

'Hmm. Yes, he does indeed.'

'While you two chat, I'll get us a drink,' Peter said. 'What would you like, Fiona?'

'A white wine would be good thanks.'

'Anything for you, Ivy?'

'No thanks, Pete. I'm on a cleanse,' Ivy said.

The doctor nodded and disappeared into the crowd.

'What do you do for a living, love?' Ivy asked her.

'I write features for magazines,' Fiona said.

'Do you now? Any magazines I might know?'

'Only if you love business.'

Ivy smiled. 'Not at all.'

Fiona returned her smile. 'What do you do?'

'I'm a psychologist. Peter and I often consult for each other, actually.'

'I see. It must be interesting work,' Fiona said.

'It is. Challenging though. People on the land don't open up readily.'

'No, I suppose not,' Fiona thought of Alick. She doubted he was the type to share his innermost fears, but then neither was she.

The conversation stalled at that point. Fiona and Ivy stood about with their hands hanging loose at their sides like people do when they have nothing in common. Finally, Peter returned with two glasses of wine. He handed Fiona one.

'Let me show you around, Fiona. It's an amazing old building. You don't mind, do you Ivy?'

'No, of course not. You two enjoy yourselves.'

Ivy winked at Peter and Fiona took a large swallow of her wine. She followed the doctor through the centre of the hall toward the rear. They passed a small room with a long table where food was being prepared. The ceiling was much lower there and appeared to be an enclosed rear porch. Peter pointed out the ceiling. 'This is the only surface in the place not made out of local timber. Asbestos,' he said. 'Nasty stuff. The proceeds from this evening will go a long way toward removing it safely and replacing it with –'

'With timber, I imagine,' Fiona said.

Peter smiled. 'How did you guess?'

'Do you mind if we get another drink?' Fiona asked him. She felt brittle. The alcohol would soothe her.

At the bar, she was introduced to more people. They swirled into her vicinity and out again, all welcoming, all polite. She forgot most of their names immediately, except for the butcher, Arthur Sweeney.

'Call me Art,' the big man said, pumping her hand with his three-fingered one.

'Art,' she mimicked, as pain travelled up to her elbow.

'Is the old man making you feel welcome, Fiona?' he asked with a sideways grin.

Fiona smiled back. 'Not in an overly obvious way.'

Art spluttered and his beer dribbled down the front of his shirt. 'Good one, young lady. That's a real good one! Come by and I'll do you a good deal on some top-quality meat.'

'I will. I promise.' Fiona went to take another drink and found her glass empty.

'Let me get you another of those,' Art said.

The lights on their long cords swung above her and the walls tilted.

❋

'It's beautiful steak. Didn't I tell you lad?' Harry said, wiping a hand across his mouth and then patting his stomach.

Alick turned away to get another beer, so they would not see him smile. Harry was lucky he hadn't shot him when he turned up out of the blue. People normally had enough sense to stay away. Alick knew the boy was a drawcard. It was not like he and Harry would sit alone together and shoot the breeze, but with the boy, Sven, as a buffer, Harry could direct all his questions to him and Alick could sit idly by. There was something not altogether uncomfortable in that.

'Tell us about your family,' Harry said. 'The old man said you're from Sweden.'

'Yes,' the boy said. 'From Sweden. Family from Sweden.'

Alick eased himself down on the old wooden bench seat across from the BBQ.

'Are your parents still over there?' Harry asked. 'In Sweden, I mean.'

'In Sweden,' the boy agreed.

Alick wondered what it would be like to travel the world as the boy did. When he was a lad, he had imagined doing just that, but the war had come instead.

'What part of Sweden are you from?' Harry asked. The vet was leaning forward and talking loudly as if this would make him better understood.

The boy looked shaken.

'Christ Harry! Shut up, will you? He thinks you're a nutter,' Alick growled.

'Just being friendly, Alick,' the vet said. 'Sorry lad.'

Alick had to give it to Harry. He was a friendly bloke. It seemed he couldn't help himself. Unlike most people, he never took offence, even when Alick meant to give it. It was as if he had no ache inside him.

✷

Fiona was perched on one of the horizontal log barriers which separated the car park from the grassy space in front of the hall. She was staring at her shoes and had been for quite some time when a pair of black loafers entered her field of vision.

'Want some company?'

Fiona knew it was Peter before she looked up and sidled along the log to make room for him. Actually, she did want company. It had occurred to her just how drunk she was and how raw she felt.

'Things are winding up inside,' Peter said. 'You must have been out here for a while.'

She nodded. It was true. She had been fine. Talking and laughing with the locals and then suddenly she wasn't. She knew she should have paced herself. Had some water maybe. Talked more than she had drunk, but there had been things to cover over, smooth out, and make her more presentable.

'Are you cold?' Peter asked.

'No, no. Just a little drunk, I think.'

Regardless, Peter moved closer to her and Fiona felt unexpectedly grateful. She felt all of his presence through their touching shoulders and she drew from that small point of intersection. She felt it as a tingling. It pulsed down her arm to her hand in one direction and across her shoulder and into her chest in the other. It seemed primitive to her, a sharing of a species, a doctoring for her loneliness. Did he feel it too?

'Is everything all right?' Peter asked.

Fiona straightened, breaking the physical contact. 'Yes, I'm fine.'

'Shall we go, then?'

'Yes, yes.' Fiona pushed herself to her feet. Her head swirled, and Peter placed an arm under her elbow for support.

The drive to her house was executed in silence. Fiona realised how tired she was. The passing paddocks and the curves in the road lulled her into a weird dream state. Cows, fences, road signs and people hung suspended on a background of black, like portraits. Fiona could do nothing more than watch this absurd gallery flicker past her. 'Gwendolyn with Cow.' 'Richard with Fencepost.'

Peter brought the four-wheel drive to a halt outside the empty farmhouse. The silence stung her. She felt a soft pressure on her wrist, then a gentle shaking. Fiona opened her eyes.

'We are here.'

She focused on the voice. She felt Peter's hand brush up her arm and his fingers stroke her neck.

'I enjoyed tonight,' he said.

His fingers caressed her ear.

'I hope you enjoyed it too,' he added.

She turned toward him, intending to reply, but kissed him instead. She needed his warmth because she had none of her own. Fiona closed her eyes again and felt a stranger's hands on her body.

SHOOTING UP

Fiona woke with a thick pulse in her neck. The glare from the window was painful to behold and yet she was calm and distinctly within herself. There was no bleeding around her edges. She stretched her arms above her head and her body was long and liquid. She remembered the strangeness of Peter's hands. The fluttering of them in ways not known before, the trill of them up and down her spine. How dissimilar sex could be. Not better or worse. She had not reached a point where she could say yet, but it could be remarkably different. She hadn't known this. She may never have known it, because Richard was her first.

The house was silent without Lochie and Hugh, who would not return until that afternoon. Fiona made tea and took it out onto the verandah. The air was cool. The world felt new. All is not lost, she thought, and hope, illusive until now, warmed her. She dressed, grabbed her keys and took off into town to buy chickens for Hugh's birthday.

She saw the young man up ahead and was almost past him when she realised it was Sven. Fiona pulled the car over on the verge. 'Are you going into town?'

Sven nodded.

'Would you like a lift?'

'Yes, thank you,' he said, in his polite English. He settled in the seat beside Fiona and she drove on.

She peered furtively at her passenger. He looked young, not much older than Hugh, but she knew this could not be so. She studied the line of his jaw, the wide straight mouth, and the heavy-lidded blue eyes staring down the road. He sat still in the seat as if she weren't there. One hand remained on the soft handle of a small backpack, while the other rested curled in his lap. She thought him composed, except that wasn't quite it. There was a readiness to him.

'Are you living on the farm now?' she asked him.

'I camp. I have a tent,' he replied, staring ahead though the windshield.

'I thought you would be staying in the house,' she said.

'No.'

'But you help out on the farm?'

'Yes.'

'That's good of you,' Fiona said.

The young man nodded, but said nothing more about this.

'So, how long have you been travelling in Australia?' she asked, changing tack.

Sven's gaze slid to her. 'Almost one year.'

'Right,' she nodded. 'So, where have you visited?'

'Lots of places ... Melbourne, Sydney, Hobart, Brisbane, Alice Springs, Darwin,' he answered, awkward over the pronunciation of the names.

'Wow. That's quite an adventure,' she said.

'Yes,' he said, looking down the road again.

Fiona drove into town and pulled into a parking space across from the doctor's surgery. The doors were shut tight.

'I need to go in there,' she said, gesturing toward the pharmacy, 'but I'm wondering if you could help me after?'

The boy looked straight at her for the first time, but his expression was blank, and she couldn't tell whether he understood her. Still, she continued on. 'I was planning to buy some live chickens for the pen at the farmhouse. If you help, I can drive you back.'

Sven looked at his feet, appearing to consider her proposal and then up again. 'I will help,' he nodded. 'I will buy my food and come back here.'

Fiona watched him walk across the road toward the supermarket, his shoulders drawn high and his arms held stiffly at his sides, as if he still carried the weight of his large pack.

✳

People stood chatting, forming a bottleneck near the fruit and vegetable bins and in an alcove between a fridge displaying lines of milk and one with cheeses. They didn't move aside when others approached. This was unnecessary. The newcomers would often stop too. They would listen for a time and pluck up the thread of the conversation, while those among them, who had paused longest, would move on. From a bird's-eye view the movement was intricate, the colours kaleidoscopic.

A young man slipped through the gaps and moved stealthily up and down aisles. At first, he went unnoticed. His fair head bobbed and darted. However, in the aisle where one could find the curious combination of sun hats and soup, he caught the attention of Margaret, whose job it was to keep the shelves filled with produce. She noted the depth of the pockets in his army green jacket. She appraised the meagre contents of his basket and saw that, while he seemed to be interested in Aisle 3, there was nothing in the basket which had originated there. She also knew the lone security camera, located down by the paint-by-numbers craft shelf, hadn't worked in months.

Sven became aware of Margaret, while deciding between Tomato and French Onion soups. From the corner of his eye, he noted she was looking him over from out of the corner of hers. He took down a can of Roast Pumpkin soup and placed it in his basket.

Margaret ceased her sideways glances and faced him. She smiled and nodded and moved past him, pushing her large platform on wheels laden with bulk packs of dried dog food. Sven waited until she had disappeared around the corner at the end of the aisle before returning the can to the shelf and slipping a two-pack of French Onion soup into a pocket.

A prolonged observation of Sven's shopping behaviour would not provide a clue to what went into his pockets and what he chose for his basket. His decisions were not based on size, price, or on fresh foods vs packaged items. By the time he reached the checkout, the contents of both pockets included the soup, four Cherry Ripes, some ham wrapped in paper from the deli, a packet of sausages, a block of cheese, Jatz biscuits and two apples, positioned one each side for balance. In his basket, were a packet of razors, hamburger patties, a tomato, a small notebook and a ballpoint pen. He stood in line refusing the offer to use the self-service section. From experience, the attendants who monitored the pay stations were cannier and more likely to brush against him.

A pale-faced gamer type with eyes like a lizard manned his checkout. He blinked at Sven from time to time, as he weighed and scanned his purchases. Margaret walked by him. Sven nodded to her as he handed over one of notes Alick had given him in exchange for the removal of the dead cow.

The woman was waiting by the car when Sven returned.

'Would you like to put your shopping bags in the car and then we can get the chickens?' she asked, miming the placing of the bags in the open boot.

He nodded and stowed his purchases, using the lid of the car's boot for cover while he emptied his pockets into the bags.

At the produce store, a fat storekeeper came out from behind his counter and offered his hand to Fiona. 'I remember you from the other day,' he said. 'You were in with your two younger boys.'

Sven understood the storekeeper believed he belonged to the woman.

'Yes,' she said, clasping the storekeeper's hand and giving it a quick shake.

'I'm Jim,' the storekeeper added.

'I'm Fiona and this is Sven,' she said.

Sven bowed his head a little and said in his thickest accent, 'Hello.'

'Oh, so not your son then?' Jim asked, looking from Fiona to Sven and back to Fiona again.

Sven stood very still beside Fiona. He felt her stiffen, as if a line had been crossed for her too. He looked away and pretended to study the store.

'No, Sven is a friend, a neighbour,' Fiona said. 'We have come to buy some chickens.'

'Ahh,' Jim said. 'Would that be point-of-lay chickens, madam?' The storekeeper smiled winningly at Fiona.

'I don't know what that means,' she replied, abruptly.

Sven smiled inside.

Jim tugged at the collar of his shirt, aware he had mislaid his charm. 'Well, point-of-lay chickens are youngsters who will lay soon.'

Fiona considered this. 'Well, I think they are what we want.'

'Okay then. How about we get Sven here to go around the back and collect a couple of cardboard boxes to put them in?' Jim suggested to Fiona. Then, he addressed Sven directly. 'The ones with the flaps still attached.' He cocked a thumb over his shoulder to a doorway behind him.

Sven wandered through the doorway into the back of the shop. He had pinned the woman as a middle-class snob. Just knowing that the store owner had pissed her off too made him like her more. To the side of a large loading dock, he found a random assortment of boxes thrown into a musty corner. There had been no attempt to stack them or flatten them for easier storage. Sven nodded to himself. He could see how Jim had mistaken him for the woman's son. Both he and Fiona were blonde. It was an obvious place to start. Sven knew this more than most.

The boy sits in front of the television on a filthy and dilapidated sofa with his legs bent in front of him, his arms wrapped around them, and his chin resting on his knees. It is his fourteenth birthday and he is watching a cricket match between Australia and Pakistan.

'Stevie, little Stevie, can you bring your Mummy her bottle? There's a good little boy now.'

He frowns, his gaze slides away from the television set in the direction of the bathroom and then returns again as the bowler starts his run up and the crowd clap rhythmically along. The clapping picks up the pace as the bowler gets closer and closer to the wicket.

'Stevie! Get my fucking vodka, will ya?'

He goes to the kitchen and pulls a bottle from the iced-up fridge freezer. His mother lies in the bathtub with a cigarette hanging out of the corner of her mouth. She smiles at him and the bottle, and the cigarette falls in the scummy water.

'You're my little treasure, aren't you Stevie?' She holds out her arms toward him, not bothering to hide her breasts.

Steven looks away. 'It's my birthday, Mum,' he says. 'Remember?'

'Yes, little Stevie's birthday,' she mutters, reaching out for the bottle. 'Stevie's birthday,' she says again, but he knows she isn't listening, even to herself. She is mostly gone now, the world and everything in it, including him, smudged out. A swig of vodka centres her and brings her back. She focusses on his face. 'I love you, Stevie,' she says.

Stevie hears the commentary from the cricket game rise in excitement. He knows a wicket has fallen or a boundary has been scored in his absence. 'I love you too, Mum,' he says, so he can leave, but he doesn't. He just stands there looking at her. Her white blonde hair is lank, almost colourless in the water and her pale blue eyes are red-rimmed and bare of lashes. There are gaps in her mouth where her teeth have rotted out and those which remain are brown and grey. Sores mark the skin on her arms and legs and there are more around her mouth now. Stevie knows she is more dead than alive. He knows it would have been best if she had never met his nameless father. She would have continued on her backpacking adventure and returned home to Sweden. She would have lived another life.

His mother takes another swig from the vodka bottle and he sees her eyes clear again. 'Oh Stevie,' she says. She waves a scabby arm at him. 'Do you think you could get my gear from the top drawer under the sink?'

'It's my birthday, Mum,' he whines.

'So what?' she says. 'You know your mother's got to relax.'

Steven scowled at the mass of boxes. He chose two of them with their flaps still attached and kicked away the rest to make a path back into the store. He didn't like to remember. Ambulance officers had pulled her body from the bathtub later that night and he had taken her backpack and disappeared before social services had arrived.

'There you are, son,' said Jim. 'We thought we would have to go in after you.'

Steven balled his hand into a tight fist. He wanted to break the storekeeper's nose. Instead, he attempted to hand over the boxes.

'Nah, you carry them,' Jim said dismissively, already making his way over the little ramp to the back of the store.

Steven stood, a box in each hand, his rage blossoming in his chest. He flinched when he felt a touch to his shoulder.

Fiona stood quietly beside him for a moment before easing the boxes from his grip. 'Don't worry, I'll deal with Jim,' she said.

Steven stayed where he was until he had recovered himself. Then, he strode out the back of the shop toward the bird cages.

He forced himself to study the way Jim cornered the birds, one hand swooping down to grab them by both legs. He focussed on how Jim tipped them upside down so their dangling heads could not peck him and, by the time six squawking chickens were confined in two boxes and the flaps were bent to enclose them, Steven was okay again.

*

Fiona could feel every movement of the three chickens as she walked along the street. Their feet scrabbled to keep their balance and they let out small, explosive clucks in protest. As she returned to the car, she thought of Sven, who walked alongside her with the other box. He seemed calmer, as if nothing had happened. His eyes were clear now, but they had darkened in the produce store. Richard had trained her to scan for the smallest of threats. She knew anger when she saw it.

'Hello, Fiona! Hello!' Peter stood outside his surgery waving at her across the roofs of passing cars.

Fiona paused and watched as he crossed the street toward them.

'I just wanted to say I had an enjoyable time last night,' the doctor said, smiling. Fiona looked down at his hands because she could not hold his gaze. They were long-fingered, white and sensitive-looking. Her body was not surprised. Standing on the footpath with her box of chickens, her cheeks burned. She glanced toward Sven, but he was intent on re-balancing his box.

Peter stepped closer to her and leant in. 'I was wondering if you would like to go out again. There's a lovely restaurant in Witches Falls,' he said. 'What do you think?'

She had no idea. A repeat of the previous night hadn't occurred to her. The chickens clucked. Sven shifted his weight beside her.

'We have chickens,' she said.

The chickens clucked on cue.

Peter inclined his head toward the box in her hands. 'Yes, I can hear that.'

'We need to get them home,' Fiona said.

'Yes, right. Of course.' Peter stepped away from her. 'Of course.'

Sven was the first to move off towards the car. Fiona stood for a moment and watched as the doctor retreated across the street to his surgery.

Sven had wandered off to his campsite and the chickens were huddling in the corner of the pen when Fiona's mother brought Lochie and Hugh back to the farm. It was Lochie who found Fiona first. 'Mum! We saw the mummies. They were so small. You should have seen them!'

He was right beside her when he noticed the chickens in the pen. 'You bought them,' he whispered. He held his hands on either side of his face to ward off the glare from the sinking sun and peered into the pen. 'Look Hugh,' he called out. 'Mum's got the chickens. Gran, come and see!'

Hugh came then and stood beside Lochie. The three of them watched the cowering hens.

'What are you doing out there, Fiona?' Gwendolyn called from the front path.

'Mum's bought Hugh some chickens for his birthday, Gran,' Lochie said.

Gwendolyn picked her way across the yard, stepping high on the balls of her feet as if something might bite her. 'Chickens? Why would you want chickens? They are dirty animals.'

'Mum!' Fiona said. 'Hugh thought it would be great if we produced our own eggs rather than buying them at the shop, didn't you Hugh?'

Hugh refused to save her. Instead, he arched an eyebrow at the trembling hens and sneered. 'Looks to me like you bought duds,' he said, turning back to the house.

Lochie crouched down by the pen to get a closer look. 'I don't think they are duds, Mum. I just think they are scared,' he said.

Gwendolyn's mouth had become a thin line. 'What is wrong with Hugh, Fiona?'

Fiona moved away from Lochie knowing her mother would follow her. 'There's nothing wrong,' she said.

Gwendolyn drew in a sharp breath. 'Don't you think it's about time you and Richard reconciled? The boys need stability. Your father and I have said nothing until now, but we are worried about Hugh. Lochie too, for that matter.'

Fiona watched the shadows from the pepper tree's ferny foliage flit over her mother's blonde perm. She knew what it cost her mother to mention such things. They had never been close.

'Don't worry about it, Mum. In fact, I have been thinking of throwing a garden party for Hugh's birthday and we would love it if you and Dad could come,' Fiona said, before she had the sense to stop herself.

SKIPPING STONES

Alick woke early to Daisy pushing on the paddock gate. He must have heard the creak and bang of it over and over before it pulled him out of sleep. The old man threw back the bed covers and swung his legs to the floor. The pain in his lower back was only a twinge now and he was happy for it. He turned on the lights as he made his way down the stairs for the sun was yet to rise over the mountains.

Daisy lowed in the grey light as he approached, and she butted the gate again.

'What's the matter, old girl?' Alick slipped through the fence and patted the cow down, checking for damage. There was nothing. No heat in her udder to indicate the mastitis had returned, no wounds on her hide. She butted the gate again.

Alick stepped around the cow to inspect the water trough and found it empty. 'Bone dry,' he muttered. 'No wonder you're cranky.' He listened for the pump in the shed and heard it labouring. Alick drew water from the shed tank and splashed two bucketfuls into the trough to slake the cow's thirst before he headed toward the creek to check the intake valve.

Alick skirted Sven's campsite behind the ridge and passed the thin stream of smoke from his fire. He noted the neatness of it, the old oilskin placed at the door of the tent, a frypan with a plate and a knife and fork cleaned and stacked under the tent's small awning. The steers under the tree watched him pass, too disinterested to move. The old farmhouse was dark and quiet.

Alick breathed deeply in the slight morning chill. The walking loosened his muscles and warmed his back. He rounded the corner post and walked into the trees just as the sun broke over the back of the mountain.

Water gurgled over rocks and around the big old gums. He stepped over fallen branches and between boulders towards the deep rockpool. Spring-fed from the mountain, this was the only part of the creek which held water even in drought and this was where he had laid the pipe for the water pump. The water here was still and deeply blue. Reeds grew around the edges between the smooth rocks and dragonflies whizzed from pale dawn to shadow like tiny float planes.

The old man stood on the water's edge where the black pipe disappeared beneath the surface. The small birds twittered high in the trees and the foraging bush turkeys rustled about in the leaf litter. He felt younger here. He saw his child-self jumping from rock to rock, a stick held as a rifle, nimble on his bare feet. Alick's childhood was filled with fresh air, leaves and mud and water, but as an only child he'd played here alone. He'd needed to imagine his band of warriors and his foe. It had been real to him, more real than if the other children had been flesh and blood and intent on their own adventures.

Alick propped his rifle against a tree. He bent at the waist and selected a smooth flat rock from the creek's edge, the size of a fifty-cent piece. He tossed it up and down in his hand a few times to feel its weight, drew his arm back and, with a flick of his wrist, sent it skimming across the still water. It skipped once ... twice ... three times and Alick smiled.

'You are very good at that.'

He heard a rustle and turned to see the woman from the farmhouse sitting cross-legged at the base of one of the large camphor laurel trees. He acknowledged her with a nod.

'You grew up here, didn't you?' she asked him. 'You must know this place very well.'

Alick nodded again.

The woman rose and selected her own stone. He watched her throw it into the pool and saw it sink.

Alick picked up another, again flat and polished by the water. He showed her the wrist action needed to spin the stone but did not release it. Instead, he handed it to her.

She drew back her wrist and sent the stone out over the water. It skipped once ... twice. She smiled at him. 'Thank you,' she said. 'I will practise.' Then, she walked back through the trees toward the old farmhouse.

Alick stood beside the creek for a long time. He felt the woman's presence still, even though he knew her to be gone. He sat on the cool dark soil beside the creek to remove his boots. He rolled his trousers up above his skinny knees and prepared for the shock of the cold water. Alick took a deep breath and lowered his legs over the edge of the creek bank. He had a pump to prime.

❋

The stone spun through the air and skipped across the deep water of the creek. She and the farmer watched it. Something dead made to look alive. Like me, she thought.

Fiona mumbled something to Alick and turned away quickly so he would not see her cry.

At the farmhouse, she veered from the path toward the chicken pen nestled inside the elbow of the fence line and still deeply shaded. 'They will be fine tomorrow morning.' This is what she told herself, when even Lochie had given up on the chickens and gone inside. But they weren't fine. She could see the little hillocks of their vibrating bodies grounded still, too terrified to perch.

She slumped down onto the garden edging. Her purchase of psychologically damaged chickens was further evidence of her poor judgement, and it had come just in time to remind her that hope was a mirage.

Only the day before she had felt substantial after her dalliance with the doctor. She was solid again, as if in moving against him, she had emerged from a fog and parried a blow against invisibility. But this was not to last. Peter had asked her out again, while she and Sven held boxes of chickens in the street and her fragmented self had returned. Then, right here by the chicken pen, Gwendolyn had oozed disappointment and Fiona's only response was to invite her to a birthday party she was sure Hugh didn't want.

Fiona could recognise melodrama when she saw it. She recognised its edge, the border between self-control and a plummet into thin air. She knew that line like she knew nothing else. It had taunted her for months now. When most of what she believed proved false and the rules had dissolved, she had that line. But on the back of this latest error in judgement, she crossed it. She clasped her arms around her bent knees and placed her head on top of them. She sighed a sigh so deep, even Gwendolyn may have been jealous.

As it was, there was no one to see Fiona's funk and for this she was grateful. She sighed again and again. She felt the ache of self-pity expand her chest and the pressure of tears build. She took in more air and the sigh was ragged this time. In that small world encompassed by her head on folded arms and bent knees, she understood she had become habitually terrified. The fear was always there, and it took everything she had to keep it at bay. It took a line, drawn so long ago, to keep her walking and talking and doing as expected. And while she was acknowledging the true depth of her dysfunction, she heard rustling. Fiona raised her forehead from her arms. Her scene of despair had not gone unnoticed. Six sets of unwavering black eyes stared back at her, and in their gaze, Fiona saw the only question worth posing, 'Who's the mentally incompetent one now?'

A laugh broke from her and one by one the chickens rose above their terror and stretched on spindly legs. The food thrown the previous evening to incentivise them materialised and they began to peck cautiously and then with increasing vigour.

'I'm sorry about the other day. I didn't understand,' Fiona said.

'I don't know what you mean. What was there to understand?' Peter asked, clearly perplexed.

Fiona gripped her phone tighter. She knew he was referring to the practice of following one successful date with another. 'I didn't realise that you might want to see me again.'

He laughed then. 'Why ever not? I think we can safely say we both had a good time.'

Fiona had no idea what she could safely say and so she said, 'Yes.' In any case, more sex was needed to stiffen her spine.

'Good. I'm glad that's settled,' Peter said, as if it was his mission to go about settling things. 'As I mentioned yesterday, there is a lovely restaurant up at Witches Falls. It has a nice fireplace, very cosy.'

Fiona knew it. She had visited it once with Richard on a weekend away.

＊

The pressure had been building all week. Fiona saw it in Hugh's stony face and felt it in the car going to and from the school bus stop. It caused frisson when they brushed by each other in the house, but she had carried on despite this. She had been a juggernaut. She still was. She plunged toward Hugh's birthday party with grim determination, all the while dismissing the understanding which squatted inside her. No good could come of it.

Finally, the pressure was released when Fiona asked Hugh to hang balloons on the verandah on the morning of the party.

'I know why you are doing this,' he said.

Tell me, she pleaded inside her head. To Hugh, she said, 'We are celebrating your birthday.'

'No, you're not,' Hugh answered her. 'This has nothing to do with me. You and Lochie just want to pretend. It's a big show for Grandma and Grandpa and for Aunty Julia and Uncle Graham! All of it's a show,' he said.

'So, I'll cancel it then?' she said, but Hugh was already gone. She heard the door to the sleep-out slam behind him.

Fiona dragged a chair over to a verandah post and began to hang the balloons. She forced her shaking fingers to tie the knots. Hugh was right, of course. It was for show. It had started as a means to deflect her mother and had become a sham. She wished she shared Julia's way with their mother.

Julia was kinder, more suited to the role. Her mother and her sister gave each other the space they needed, while Fiona and Gwendolyn grated against one another. Her mother loved her, yes, but couldn't like her.

Fiona studied her sad balloons. She caught sight of the farmer on the ridge above the farmhouse. He stood as she had seen him on that first day with his rifle resting on his hip, looking down the paddock toward his cows. She nodded to him, a salute of sorts, even though she knew he couldn't see her.

❋

The sound floated to him, as Alick walked the ridge. Another peal of laughter sprang up like a sudden squall and the old farmer grimaced. He was not one for parties. Even so, he dropped onto his stomach and brought his rifle to bear on the scene. Through the scope, he watched as the woman came out of the house carrying a plate of food. He knew the shape of her now. He centred his scope on her face first and then did the same with the six people sitting around the table on the verandah. He noted a likeness between the women, the chin and the eyes. Alick felt an ache in his chest.

'Most young men are trying to avoid the draft and you go and enlist,' his mother says to him, caring nothing for the rise of communism. She thinks for a minute. She tilts her chin upward, her gaze intent on the ceiling. This is a breakfast table conversation, as all important ones are in Alick's family, and his mother's tilting and staring is a signal to stay put and await her verdict. Alick looks across to his father, who is present in the most minimal of ways. His conversation over Alick's enlistment has already occurred. It consisted of a look from his father, when they were walking the fences to the property. Worry had been there, Alick knew, but there was also admiration. Though he will never say it, Alick knows his father is proud. He believes in sacrifices to protect family and country. Alick is sliced with guilt every time he recognises he is hiding behind this false virtue to escape the farm. He much prefers to endure his mother's forced family meetings than to feel a liar in his father's presence.

Alick looks back to his mother who, with a series of frowns and sighs, seems near to a conclusion.

'You are an idiot,' she says, releasing her visual grip on the ceiling and pinning him to the chair with her gaze. He knows she suspects the truth. He feels her sense of betrayal, but he also sees that she understands.

✳

'This steak is amazing,' Graham said, slicing off another piece and inspecting it. 'It is, isn't it Julia?'

'Yes, darling.' Julia smiled at Fiona across the table. 'Thanks, Fi.'

They were sitting around the old kitchen table which had been relocated to the verandah that morning. Fiona sat in a patch of sunlight, while the conversation washed over her. She could have curled up like a cat and slept.

'You must have a great butcher in that little town on the way out here,' Fiona's father commented. 'They are hard to come by. Perhaps your mother and I should pop in on the way back.'

Fiona stirred. There was too much talk of meat, but she took too long to respond.

'It's the farmer's cow,' Hugh muttered. 'He shot it by accident.'

'What do you mean, sweetie?' Gwen asked, leaning across the table toward Hugh, who hadn't said a thing to anyone since the party began.

'He was up on that ridge there,' Hugh said, pointing.

Fiona watched as her parents swivelled in their chairs to take in the ridge. Graham and Julia looked too.

'What happened then?' Stuart asked Hugh.

'Well, he just dropped onto to his stomach and shot at the cows under the tree. One of them fell over ... dead.'

'How awful,' Gwen said, placing her hand over her mouth in horror.

Silence fell and, one by one, they turned to Fiona.

'It's an odd thing to do, don't you think?' her father asked her.

'I warned her about farmers and guns,' Gwendolyn said. 'Didn't I tell you he was dangerous, Fiona?'

Fiona still didn't answer. She was watching Hugh. She saw him smirk at her discomfort and her spirits fell. They were divided, she and Hugh. He no longer trusted her.

'Fiona?' her mother prompted her again.

Fiona shrugged. 'You are making too much of this,' she said. 'So, what if he shot a cow.'

'But he didn't shoot it deliberately, love,' her father said. 'It sounds like he might have some problems.'

Suddenly, her father's reasonableness irritated her. 'So what? We all have problems, don't we?' she said.

'Well ... yes,' Stuart said.

'And the meat is real good,' Lochie added. 'We are farmers too, Grandpa. You should see our chooks and

Hugh's garden. We will be able to give you eggs and vegetables soon.'

'That's wonderful, Lochie,' Stuart said, shooting Fiona a look which told her the topic would be raised again. 'I'd love to see your chickens and Hugh's garden.'

As soon as Fiona and Julia were alone, Fiona's sister said, 'What the hell, Fi?'

They were in the kitchen washing the dishes while Graham was tinkering with the sticky screen door. 'He accidentally shot his own cow?'

'Yes,' Fiona said.

'Aren't you worried he might shoot you or one of the boys?'

Fiona looked away from the pile of dirty plates, taking in Julia's concern. Then she gazed out the small kitchen window and shrugged. She could feel her sister studying her.

'You know you are getting weirder,' Julia said. 'A lot weirder, little sister.'

Fiona smiled. 'I know.'

'Well,' Julia said, pushing herself away from the kitchen bench with both hands, 'I'll go out and check on Mum and Dad and the kids, shall I?'

'Sure.'

Fiona washed the rest of the dishes while listening to Graham bang on the door. She took up a tea towel and began to dry them, placing the dishes one by one back where they belonged.

'We are going, darling,' her father said, poking his head around the corner from the hall.

'Okay, I'll come and see you off,' she said, hanging the damp dishtowel while he waited for her.

'I'm worried about you,' he said, placing an arm around her shoulders as they walked down the hall toward the front verandah.

'Don't, I'm fine. There is nothing to worry about.'

Stuart stopped suddenly. 'Do you think I should go and speak to this farmer?' he asked her. 'Just to check him out, so to speak?'

Fiona was flummoxed. 'No Dad. Why?'

Stuart dropped his arm from her shoulder and looked at his shoes. 'It's just that now Richard has gone ... It's up to me to protect you.'

Fiona knew her father was a good man, an honourable one. She looked at him. His was a face she loved, but the skin around his jaw sagged now and there were deep groves in his forehead. He looked old, discouraged and she knew he could never know that it was Richard she was most frightened of. 'It's okay, Dad. Alick is not a threat. I promise I will tell you if I'm ever worried about him.'

'All right darling, I'm going to hold you to that,' Stuart said.

'Hey, on a brighter note, would you look after Hugh and Lochie next weekend?' she asked him.

'Alright,' her father said. 'Another networking event, then?'

'Yes, that's right.'

'You really should be asking your mother. She is the one who does all the work, Fiona,' Stuart said.

'Yes, I know, but I don't think now would be a good time,' Fiona said.

Stuart smiled at her. 'You might be right about that.' They stood for a moment in the hall together. Stuart raised an arm and patted Fiona in small circles on her upper back, while they stared down the dark hallway into the glare outside. The motion of his hand was an old one, something he had done when she was small and needed comfort. But it was she who had seen his vulnerability, his need to protect them and his fear that he could not. Finally, they moved outside. She stood by the track, waving to her parents as they drove away and Lochie took Julia to see the chickens.

Her mobile phone was ringing when Fiona returned to the house. She swept past Graham who had taken the screen door from its hinges and was sanding one edge of it.

'Your phone's ringing,' he said.

Fiona grabbed at it. She had had enough and wanted the day over. She wanted Graham to stop banging on the door and for he and Julia to get in their car and drive away. 'Hello,' she said.

'I want to speak to my child on his birthday,' Richard said.

Fiona willed herself to breathe, while her stomach fell inside her. Fuck him, just fuck him, she thought. 'Well, you can't speak to him, Richard,' she said.

'Are you telling me you won't let me talk to my son on his birthday?' Richard seemed incredulous, but Fiona knew he was play-acting. He loved a fight.

'Hugh doesn't want to talk to you at all,' she said.

Richard snorted. 'I thought you'd drive a wedge between us. That's what all you bitch women do, isn't it?' he snarled. 'Well, I'm not having it, so consider this your warning. I will be suing for full custody of the boys and I expect I will win.'

Fiona felt this as a punch in her chest. 'You can't,' she screamed.

Richard laughed at her panic. 'I can and I will.'

Fiona heard the click on the line before she could reply. The telephone was gently prised from her hand and an arm guided her to a kitchen chair. Graham's face came in close to her own.

'I'll get Julia,' he said.

Fiona heard his steps fade down the hall and her sister's steps return. She allowed herself to be taken into a hug.

'What did he say?' Julia asked.

'He wants custody of Hugh and Lochie,' Fiona said.

'Over my dead body,' Julia said.

'Shhh, we can't do this now while the boys are here, Jules. We just can't.'

TEASING COX

Steven pressed his shoulder into Daisy's flank as he'd seen Alick and Harry do. A cow can't kick you, if she can't see you. That's what the vet had said. Steven felt the muscles in the cow's belly and haunch bunch as he slid the milking pail under her.

'That's it, lad,' Alick said. 'Just take her high on the teat and squeeze the milk down.'

Steven took hold of the rubbery teats and squeezed. Daisy billowed a leg out to the side, just missing Steven's hip.

'No, boy,' Alick said. 'It's a gentle motion – firm but gentle. Gent-le,' he said, drawing out the word as people often did with him. The old man mimed the pulling down of the teat for Steven. 'Firm, but gent-le,' he said again.

Steven kept his face blank. It helped confirm him as a foreigner. It allowed him to fail, if he needed to. The old man would give in. Everyone did, eventually. But Steven didn't want to fail this time. He had discovered he liked cows. He liked the depth in their brown eyes, their smell and the warmth of their bodies, the velvety softness of their muzzles.

So, he took hold of one of Daisy's teats and pulled down, gently, but firmly. A stream of warm milk drilled into the bottom of the bucket. Steven smiled to himself.

'That's it, lad!' Alick said.

Steven kept milking, even when Alick wandered away to the shed. He watched the milk roll across the metal bottom of the bucket and join with the other creamy white pools. He built up a rhythm, pulling on one teat and then the other and the bottom of the bucket disappeared beneath the frothing milk. Steven felt Daisy's muscles relax, so much so, he realised she was resting a little of her weight on his shoulder. Steven felt a swelling in his chest. He'd known nothing of animals. He trusted nobody.

'That's enough, boy,' Alick said. 'The bucket's full.'

Steven stilled his hands but stayed just a little longer with his shoulder pressed into Daisy.

'Just hand over the bucket and I'll put it in the jug for chilling. My mother used to make a wonderful rice pudding with the fresh milk,' Alick muttered.

The old man did this sometimes. He'd say these random things, which he thought Steven couldn't understand.

The young man did as he had done before. He waited for the moment to pass.

'You can let her go now,' Alick said, pointing to Daisy's halter.

Steven stood and moved to the cow's head. He heard the creak of the paddock gate and the rattle of the chain which secured it. He listened for the old farmer's receding steps. Steven petted the cow on her soft brown muzzle. 'Good girl, Daisy. Good girl,' he said. He wanted her to know his true voice.

✻

'Look, it depends on how you define bullying, doesn't it love?' said Jeremy Cox, the vice president of Wallis Industries.

Fiona drew in a breath and exhaled slowly. Renee Rodgers had warned her. 'No, no, it doesn't actually. Bullying has been defined very clearly by the courts and by government, so no, that's not correct at all.'

Cox cleared his throat. 'Listen here, miss. There are always a couple of disgruntled employees in any organisation. You can take that to the bank.'

Cox's attitude infuriated Fiona. She now had him firmly in her sights. 'Okay Mr Cox, let me ask my question in another way. Excluding the out-of-court settlements, past and future –'

'I'm not at liberty to discuss those,' Cox cut in.

'Yes, I know that, Mr Cox. That is why I am excluding them. The withdrawals would be high, wouldn't they?' Fiona asked.

'What do you mean, withdrawals?' Cox asked in a strangled voice.

'Withdrawals from the bank you mentioned, erosion of profit margins ... however you like to put it, Mr Cox.'

Cox made noises as if to interrupt, but Fiona continued on. She knew he would soon hang up and there was little point pursuing him with nothing of substance to support her claims. 'I mean, with the retraining of offenders, the loss of good employees fleeing a toxic workplace, and the lost time in production, wouldn't that mean the costs to Wallis Industries are much higher than first anticipated?' Cox attempted to butt in again, but Fiona continued. Something in her needed him to squirm. 'I have a copy of a study done in the UK, which shows the strategy of settling without addressing the issue of bullying will become a thing of the past, due to the very real effects bullying has on the bottom line. Would you like to comment on that, Mr Cox?'

Cox spluttered into the phone. 'No, I would not. '

'Would you like me to send you a copy of the UK study, Mr Cox?'

'Who are you? Which paper do you work for again?'

'My name is Fiona Lees, Mr Cox. Not 'love' or 'miss', and I don't work for a paper. I write in-depth features for *In Business* magazine and we do our research.' The phone clicked in her ear as Jeremy Cox hung up.

Regret flooded in. She should not have baited Cox. It was wildly unprofessional. Fuck! She had to get her shit together. On top of this, the story was a good one, but what she had gotten so far wasn't strong. Fiona took her phone out onto the verandah and rang her editor.

Steph answered immediately.

'Do you have time to talk about the bullying story?' Fiona asked.

'Sure, just let me shut the door. I have a new policy with Padma. If the door is shut, it means leave me the fuck alone.'

Fiona smiled. 'Is it working?'

'Not particularly well, no,' Steph sighed.

Fiona heard Steph's door slam shut.

'Right, so what's up?' Steph asked.

Fiona sat on the stairs in a patch of sunlight. 'I've just spoken to a Jeremy Cox from Wallis Industries which, according to Renee Rodgers, has a terrible track record when it comes to bullying. I get the feeling it's pretty entrenched over there.'

'Why do you think that?' Steph asked.

'Cox put the allegations down to a few disgruntled employees. He was offhand, like he was in no danger of being held to account.'

'Okay and I'm guessing you didn't have enough to counter the argument?'

'No. I thought he would want to hide the evidence; that he wouldn't want to talk about it at all,' Fiona said, realising how stupid she had been.

'You thought you would get a bunch of no comments then?' Steph said.

'I did. I didn't think he'd openly blame the victims because I didn't think he would admit there were any.'

'Really? Come on, Fiona. Victim-blaming is one the most effective ways to slip the noose. Say they are troublemakers, crazies or liars and you are halfway to getting away with it. It seems plausible and it's easier for people to accept than the possibility the victims are telling the truth.'

Fiona knew Steph was right. Her editor was razor-sharp. 'Okay, so I need to talk to a victim, don't I?'

'You do. Otherwise you will have to write it up and move on.'

'Right.'

'Well, good luck with it. I've got to go.' The line went dead.

Fiona walked down the steps. She stood in the middle of the yard. It would be a shame if this story went nowhere. She didn't want it to be like every other story on bullying, utterly lacking in substance and heavily reliant on statistics. She wanted it to be undeniable.

The chickens scratched around under the bushes near the old picket fence, which bordered the yard. There was no fear in them now. It was as if they had always been there, clucking and scratching. It was calming to watch them.

Fiona took a deep breath and stretched her arms above her head. She would ring Renee Rodgers on the off-chance she could help, but she knew it was a big ask.

Fiona's phone buzzed in her hand and Julia's name glowed on the display. She stared at it, letting the call ring out. Fiona knew Julia wouldn't stop ringing until they had spoken about Richard.

*

'Do you like them?' Lochie asked.

Steven nodded. He did like the chickens. He had been returning from the house paddock along the track when he had heard them clucking away under the bushes by the old farmhouse. Initially, he watched from beyond the fence. Fiona was watching too. She had stood in the middle of the yard with her arms above her head, had twirled once and then jumped when her phone rang. He had jumped as well, but the chickens had clucked on happily. Once she had left, he drew closer, until he was sitting on the grass in the yard with his knees bent and his arms wrapped around them, just watching. This was how the little boy had discovered him.

Lochie stood by him for a while, watching the chickens too. 'They are cool, aren't they? And very friendly,' he said.

Steven nodded.

'You can touch one if you like.' Lochie picked up a hen and cradled it in one arm, bringing it closer.

Steven reached out his hand and touched the feathers. They were stiffer than he expected. The chicken clucked softly.

'Would you like to hold it?' the boy said.

Steven nodded again and Lochie placed the bird in Steven's arms. He was surprised by the chicken's lightness, that underneath the feathers, the body was so small. After stretching its legs, the hen relaxed and nestled into Steven's lap.

'You see, she likes you,' Lochie said.

'I have to go now,' he said to the little boy.

'Okay, but you can come back and see them again,' Lochie said, as if he were granting Steven a great favour.

'Thanks,' Steven said, handing over the chicken and rising to his feet.

'Sven, I'll give you an egg when they start laying,' Lochie
called to him as Steven walked back along the track toward
his camp site.

MOTHER'S CHIFFONIER

Steven moved through the house. Cones of sunlight struck the floorboards like spotlights. In a room under the eaves of the verandah toward the back of the house, he found a model of a WW2 aircraft. He took it down from its shelf and ran a hand along the fuselage. The stickers bubbled under his fingertips. He knew he could have done better. He would have pushed out the bubbles with the edge of his fingernail, until the stickers lay flush. He saw himself building the model from scratch. Spotting the plastic with glue and pressing the pieces together. Painting it a silver-grey. It comforted him just to think of it.

In his mind, he would sit at a desk like the one pushed up against the louvres in this room. Fiona, or someone like her, would come down the hall and call him to dinner and he would place the tiny cap on the glue and the little lids on the paints and the model would lie undisturbed until he returned.

Steven heard a car making its way up the track. He gripped the airplane to return it to its place. It hovered in the air as airplanes do and, at the very last moment, he released it and allowed it fall to the floor. When the doors of the car creaked open outside, Steven was slipping out of the back door.

*

Knots tightened in Fiona's stomach as she sat at her kitchen table and listened to a recorded spiel of the advocacy group's services. She knew what she would be asking of Renee Rodgers and she also knew it was a long shot.

'Fiona, it's good to hear from you?' Renee's voice was bright and welcoming. 'How can I help?'

'I spoke with Jeremy Cox from Wallis Industries and I didn't get far, I'm afraid,' Fiona answered, drawing her notes from that interview toward her.

'How so?' Renee asked.

'He put the bullying complaints down to a few difficult employees and I'm afraid I had nothing to counter him with,' Fiona said. 'I need more. I need to speak with a –'

'You need to speak with a victim,' Renee cut in. 'Look Fiona, I know I don't have to tell you about confidentiality clauses, but I do need to tell you there is no way I would ever counsel a client to breach one.'

Renee's voice had taken on an edge.

'I know Renee, and I would not ask you to. Neither I or the magazine want to put your clients at risk. It's just without speaking with a victim, the story isn't strong. I'm under instruction from my editor to write up what I have and publish as is, but I just thought I'd give it one last shot.'

'Right, I'm sorry, I just don't know what to tell you,' Renee said.

Fiona closed the cover of her notebook. 'That's alright, Renee. Thanks for all your help.'

After ending the call, Fiona set about drawing up a working structure for the piece. She was considering the lead, when the door on the verandah creaked and bounced across the verandah floor.

She knew the shape of her sister before she stepped out of the dark hall and into the brightly lit kitchen.

'I see the door has returned to its natural state,' Julia said. 'Perhaps Graham should come out and take another look at it?'

'It doesn't matter,' Fiona said. She could tell by the way Julia stood with her arms hanging limp at her sides and her chin tucked into her chest she was not at all concerned about the door.

'What brings you here?' Fiona asked, breezily.

'You haven't been taking my calls. That's what brings me here. Are the boys about?' Julia asked, gazing toward the sleep-out and then Lochie's bedroom.

'No, they should be on their way to school by now,' Fiona answered. 'What's going on?'

'We are all worried about you,' Julia said.

Fiona moved to get up, but Julia laid a hand on her wrist.

'Fiona, we care, that's all.'

'Is this an intervention then?' Fiona asked, looking pointedly at their hands on the table.

'No, you know it's not, but you've got to say you've been acting pretty strangely since you left Richard and now he wants custody of the kids? You don't talk about it. You move out here and your best buddy is now a crazy old farmer who accidentally shoots his own cows? It's like you're hiding ...'

Julia came to a stop. She took a deep breath and stared at Fiona. 'You are hiding, aren't you?'

Fiona withdrew her hand from Julia's and stood. 'Do you want some lunch? I was going to have Vegemite sandwiches.'

'What?' Julia asked.

'Vegemite sandwiches. Do you want some?'

'What kind of adult still eats Vegemite sandwiches?' Julia smiled.

Fiona felt a rush of gratitude toward her sister for letting her off. 'I do, when I'm working. It's quick and it focusses the mind.'

'I'm sure it does. Okay, I'll have one.'

Fiona pulled the fresh bread from the bread box on the kitchen bench. She slowed herself and, with her back to her sister, she made lunch.

'I feel like a kid at school,' Julia said, when Fiona placed a plate of sandwiches in front of her.

Fiona smiled. 'Eat up then.'

Julia took a big bite of her sandwich and closed her eyes to chew. 'Hmm,' she murmured around the sandwich. 'I'd forgotten how good this is.'

'I know, right?' A vision floated to Fiona. Her sister was sitting across the playground with the older girls. They were laughing together, while little Fiona sat silently alongside her own classmates.

'Fi, what happened?' Julia was watching her intently.

'What do you mean?' Fiona asked, her heart hammering.

Julia frowned and Fiona knew she was losing patience with her. 'You know what I mean. What happened with Richard?'

Julia's question fell into the gap between them and Fiona felt as if she were falling with it. Her fingers and toes were numb. Her breath stilled in her lungs, caught there in a bubble with Julia's question.

'Fiona?'

Julia's face loomed in front of her, disappeared and then returned closer still.

'Fi!'

She could feel Julia gripping her hands. Something light like a silk or gossamer curtain flickered at the edge of her vision. She looked there, focussed on it and waited for it to move again, but it was gone.

'Fi!' Julia yelled.

Fiona looked to her sister. It felt as if an age had passed and Julia was a long way away. 'Julia?' Julia's hands gripped hers even harder and Fiona saw fear in her sister's face.

'Where did you go, just then?' her sister asked.

'What?' The light glowing through the window over the kitchen sink caught Fiona's attention. It soothed her.

'What just happened, Fi?'

Fiona followed her sister's voice and found Julia had pulled a chair closer to sit beside her.

'I don't know,' Fiona said.

Julia leaned forward and gave her an awkward sitting hug. It was not something they were prone to as sisters. Fiona sat still and waited.

'Could it have been a panic attack?' Julia whispered in her ear.

Fiona withdrew from the hug. Perhaps, she thought.

'I'll make some tea, shall I?' Julia suggested.

Fiona nodded.

Julia floated over near the kettle. 'How long have you been having these ... attacks?'

For so many years. For as long as ... 'Only recently,' Fiona said.

'Right. Is it money? Are you okay for money?' Julia asked, bringing the cups of tea to the table and sitting across from Fiona.

'I'm fine for money,' Fiona said. This wasn't entirely true, but it wasn't the problem.

'What brought it on? Do you know?' Julia asked, taking a sip of her tea.

Fiona did know. She'd always known. 'I don't know,' she said.

'Well, I think it's pretty normal when people split up ... to have some problems,' Julia said.

Fiona nodded.

'Well, if Richard thinks he can take the children, he will have to fight with both of us,' Julia said. 'You have to promise me you'll get a lawyer. I'll come with you, if you like.'

'Yes. I'll get a lawyer, Jules. I promise.' Julia was at her best when she was practical. The world made sense to her.

✳

Alick listened for the screech of the chainsaw and heard it rise shrill through the trees by the creek. He nodded, as he pulled open the door to the storage room at the end of the shed. The lad was handy. Picked things up quickly, he had to admit.

Inside, cobwebs hung from the rafters and daylight pierced the rusted holes in the exterior walls. Dust swirled on a small draught from the open door. Alick hesitated on the threshold. He had not been inside for a long time. As his eyes adjusted, he made out the contours of his mother's dressing table. The large mirror at the back was cracked and one of its broken side mirrors hung sadly. An ache in his chest swelled at the extent of his neglect. He averted his eyes and moved toward a corner in search of a dining-room chair. He had been thinking he could use another chair, a more comfortable one. Maybe a better armchair too. His back was not what it was.

He moved between the islands of stacked furniture, touching here and there a table, a sideboard, the kitchen chiffonier. The deep honey of the wood showed through the dust where he ran his finger over it. He saw it as it once was in the kitchen of the old farmhouse, with the plates lined up behind the thin dowel, his mother's soup tureen centred on the top shelf. Alick positioned it theoretically in his own house against the wall leading into the dining room. It would do nicely. Sven could help him move it in, he thought.

Alick located the dining chairs in the far corner atop the old dining table. Off to the side stood his father's winged chair. It was upholstered in a heavy brocade. As a child, Alick would stroke the silky indentations in the fabric. Even at a distance, he could almost feel it on his fingertips – the fur of the velvet, the cool slipperiness of the grooves. His heart fluttered with his imagined fingers.

'Alick!'

'In here,' he called out, his voice catching in a dry throat. The lad came to stand beside him in the half light. He smelt of fresh wood shavings.

'Have you finished with the wood?' Alick asked, his gaze still on his father's chair.

'Yes.'

'I'll teach you how to split it next, but I need a hand with some furniture.'

'A hand?'

'Help with the furniture,' Alick rephrased.

The lad nodded to show he understood.

Alick pointed out one dining-room chair and then decided on another for good measure. After Sven had separated out the chairs, Alick spied a small side table with a green leather top. 'This might come in handy too,' he said to Sven. On a whim, Alick pointed to the chiffonier and together they humped it to the door of the house, along the hall, and into his kitchen.

Alick stood back and looked at it. It appeared smaller in this house, almost inconsequential, dwarfed by the walls of boxes. Sven returned with a chair in each hand and placed them at the table. Alick joined him again at the shed.

'That one?' Sven asked, pointing to his father's winged chair.

'No,' Alick said. 'That can stay. Just the little table. That's all I want.'

A BAD COP

Steven is running. The darkened shops in the arcade flash by him and he knows there is no help here. He comes to the hexagonal space where the arcades converge and pauses behind the statue of the David, positioned in the centre of the mall. He is listening for the sound of footsteps. At first, he hears nothing and relief floods in, but then he hears the squeak of rubber on the marble tiles and he knows it's too late. He cannot move. He looks up at the pale, cold figure of the statue. He beseeches the statue in the manner of an ancient god. 'Hide me please.'

Instead he hears a chuckle. 'I know you are here little man.' The voice is thick and deep.

Steven's heartbeat is pulsing in his ears and he gulps at his panic. He hears the policeman take the opening to his left, which will bring him around the statue toward him. Right or left, it will not matter. In either direction, he will be discovered. He crawls on his hands and knees, keeping his head below the planter boxes of fake foliage arranged on the plinth. If he can manoeuvre himself toward the next arcade, he might make it across the open space and be flying past closed shops once more. Steven focusses on this plan. He puts his entire mind to it, and this is his mistake. He forgets to listen and with his head down he cannot see. He crawls into legs. The policeman's shoes are worn and shiny black. His terror is crushing in his chest, as a hand reaches down to grab at the collar of his shirt and raises him. His body is draped over the plinth and wedged between the planters, his bum in the air.

'Look up,' the voice commands him.

And Steven does. He is too afraid not to. He swivels his head to the side so he can see above him. The plaster penis of the David dangles over him.

'It's only right,' the voice says, and Steven feels the tug at the waistband of his board-shorts. The ripping of the Velcro fly is harsh in the silence. He feels the cool air on his buttocks and the policeman's breath hot on the back of his neck. Steven flattens his shoulders between the planter to absorb the shock to come. He is resigned now. He tells himself that stuff like this happens all the time. No street kid is immune. The lower profile of his body causes the planter to his right to shift. It scrapes across the plinth, as the police belt falls to the marble tiles.

Steven jack-knifes. His arms come around to his right, one on either side of the planter. He grips the cold concrete and continues to turn with it, his feet scrabbling for purchase on the slick floor. The corner of the planter strikes the policeman on the side of the head. He staggers and topples with his trousers around his ankles. Blood begins to pool on the grey-veined marble. Steven watches it gathering speed, as it runs into the groves between the tiles. He takes in the broken planter and the shards of it which have fallen on the policeman's chest. He sees the fake plants resting in the hollow of the policeman's bare belly, as if planted there. He sees it all like a film and then he is gone. He runs through the dark streets. He is crying and his tears whip at the corner of his eyes. He finds the bus station and he takes his key from his pocket. He opens the locker and his hands fall on his backpack. They touch the stiff fabric of it, the straps and buckles. They feel like home.

Steven woke with his shaking fingers on his pack, the dome of his tent rising above him in the gloom. Somewhere far off, a night bird called. Its cry went on and on pulling on the thread of his dream and the smashed face of the policeman hovered.

Steven slipped from his sleeping bag and out through the flap of his tent. He shuddered in the chill and wrapped himself in his oilskin coat. Out toward the east, there was little in the way of dawn. He walked along the gully, where he'd set up camp behind the ridge and climbed a small hill. The shape of the huge tree in the paddock was a black hulk. A cow snorted and shifted beneath it and a bird rustled above in its canopy. What did his history even mean before something so old? It meant nothing at all. It meant shit.

Steven returned to his camp site and urinated on the dead fire.

✳

'You know you have to,' Julia said, stridently.

Fiona imagined her sister pacing back and forth in her office, her earbuds pushed into her ears.

'Nothing is going to change otherwise. You'll be stuck in limbo.'

Fiona didn't respond. From her position by the kitchen sink, she heard Lochie open the gate to the chook pen outside and cluck to the chickens. This was comforting. Right here, this very moment was comforting. Why couldn't Julia understand that limbo wasn't so bad?

'Fiona? You don't want him to take the children, do you?' Julia asked.

'No, of course I don't.'

'I could talk to him, if you like?'

Fiona's stomach turned over. 'No, you mustn't, Julia. Not ever.'

'Are you sure? All it might take is someone with a cool head. He'll back down about the kids, I'm sure of it,' she said.

'No, he won't. You don't know what you are talking about. You just don't,' Fiona pleaded.

'Okay, okay then,' Julia said. 'You need to go to see this lawyer, then. I've heard good things about her. Very good things.'

Fiona sighed. 'Okay, I'll go.'

'Good. Pick me up at my place on Thursday and we'll go together.'

Despite her frustration, Fiona heard love in her sister's voice. She wanted to pull it around her, wrap herself in it. 'Okay,' she whispered.

Fiona slipped out through the back door. She needed fresh air and was almost to the front gate of the farmhouse when she heard Lochie whoop from the chicken pen.

'Mum!' he cried. 'They laid an egg!'

Fiona made her way back around the other side of the farmhouse to find Lochie standing triumphantly in the middle of the pen with an arm upraised. He lowered it as she approached and uncurled his fingers. On the palm of his hand sat a tiny egg.

'Isn't it awesome?' Lochie said.

'I should break it,' said Hugh, who had just arrived. 'That would teach you to stop messing around with my things.'

'I told you I didn't touch your stupid airplane,' Lochie said, turning his body away from Hugh to protect the egg.

'It's tiny anyway,' Hugh sneered. 'It's the smallest egg I've ever seen.'

'I know it's little,' Lochie said, his chin jutting back toward Hugh. 'It doesn't matter. It's still awesome.'

'Yes, it is,' Fiona agreed. 'Do you want me to cook it for you, Lochie?'

Lochie shook his head. 'It's not for me,' he said. 'I promised it to Sven.'

❋

Was it possible that a person could carry their weight in their face, but nowhere else? Fiona sat astride the doctor. His chest was well-formed. It fell away from his ribcage to the scoop of his belly. She trailed her fingers down along this curve and brushed them up again toward his chest. He quickened under her and she clasped his arm to still him. She sat back further to see more of him. All of him was as strange to her as it had been before, but this time she was better prepared. She knew that to feel a new body was not a small thing. The skin beneath her fingers held another person. It was a border she couldn't cross.

She hadn't thought this way with Richard. Their sex had been about him taking her. His penis was a means to invade her, even in the beginning when she wasn't afraid. With the doctor, she feared nothing. She felt powerful and free, floating far above and beyond Richard's control.

Fiona had known as soon as she met Peter at the restaurant, they would have sex again. Throughout dinner, she had known. After the fettuccini and the wine, she had told him she was too drunk to drive. She said he was too. Whether or not this was true, she didn't know and he didn't correct her. She had stood by while he booked the room, yearning.

And now as she shifted her weight above Peter to satisfy herself, she marvelled at the absence of fear. There was no obligation, no expectation, no threat. She rocked herself against him, faster and faster, and her body felt long and strong. She cupped his shoulders with her palms and lowered her chest closer to his to improve the angle. The tingling in her lower belly rose higher and higher.

Peter thrust again.

'No!' She hissed. 'Not yet.'

POST-COITAL DISTRUST

Alick couldn't remember when he started to consider the idea. It had grown on him and he couldn't shake free of it. It had swelled from a kernel of a thought to take on the immensity of a necessary act. Watching Sven expertly squeeze the milk from Daisy's teats made it more so.

The milk was foaming in the pail and the autumn sun warmed the back of Alick's neck. 'I fought in the Vietnam War,' he said.

Sven looked up from the milking stool. His hands paused in their rhythm.

'This was my family's property. Do you understand?'

The boy stared and then nodded. Daisy shifted position and Sven went back to his milking.

'They died, my parents, while I was at war. My father first in a tractor accident and then my mother. They say she died of a broken heart.'

Sven murmured an unknown response, his forehead buried deep in Daisy's flank.

'I didn't want to be a farmer,' Alick said, gazing to the horizon. 'I wanted to travel the world, like you. At any rate, I didn't want to die here.' Alick frowned and looked at his boots. He hadn't meant to say so much. He'd said it to avoid what he didn't have it in him to say. Alick felt his question flailing about at the back of his throat. He was always this way, when something needed saying.

Alick walks up the track toward home, his duffle bag slung on his back. He has seen many things at close quarters and at a distance through his rifle's scope. If he had intended to bring home stories of adventure, then he was wrong. There is not a thing he can say which will not lead to something unspeakable.

Alick feels the sun across his shoulders. Should he be blind, he would still know this is home. He feels the loosening grip of heat which comes with autumn. He hears the swish of the tall grass growing from the bulge of earth between the wheel-ruts in the track. There is no thundering humidity and nor is there vegetation so thick it closes off the world to spaces the size of a cowering man. He has walked this path many times. He knows no fear here. He is home.

Alick yearns for the judgmental face of his mother and the silence of his father and, as he gets closer to the farmhouse, this yearning becomes intolerable. It has played out in the corners of his mind for months now. He imagines their reunion. There will be few words spoken. He will take his mother into his arms and hold her. Then he will do the same for his father. Even though Alick knows this will shock him, he will do it anyway and keep doing it until his father is no longer shocked.

Alick mounts the stairs to the front verandah. Inside, he hears voices. He knows it is lunch time and can already see the table laid, his father sitting at its head, his hands hovering over the cutlery. Once, Alick had wondered why sandwiches wrapped in greaseproof paper and eaten on the hop were not good enough for his parents. He understands now. It is the ritual which is important. It rises above the food and forms a moment of rest in the middle of the day. Alick cannot help but marvel at his mother. He knows she maintains her marriage to a distant planet of a man by offering him what cannot be refused. Alick sees everything more clearly now.

He opens the door to the farmhouse and places his duffle bag quietly on the floor in the hall. He wants his first glimpse to be the two of them as they are before they see him. It will be a moment he holds in his memory when all else is forgotten. Alick walks the long hall toward the kitchen. On the verge of seeing them, he looks down. He adjusts his eyes for perfect focus in order to burn the next image into his heart and only then does he look up.

Old Mr Betterman sits at his parents' table. He holds a newspaper in one hand and munches on a sandwich held in the other. The radio is tuned to a talk-show. The table is not set. His hat is still pulled down on his head. This is when Alick knows his family is gone.

The old man cleared his throat and the boy looked up at him, his hands still working Daisy's udder. 'I have a room you could stay in. There's no one else using it. No rent required, just help with the farm.' He had intended to broach the subject carefully. Instead, it spilled from him all at once. Alick didn't want to see the answer on the boy's face. 'Here,' he said. He tossed Sven the keys to the truck. 'Take the afternoon off and drive into town, why don't you.'

❋

Fiona woke to a warm bed and stretched her body its full length. Her blood circulated slow as lava. Alongside her, the doctor lay curled, the curve of his spine like a knotted rope. She sat and swung her legs over the edge of the bed. Grey light filtered through a window hung with ruffled curtains and the occasional car driving the escarpment road was a muffled hum. She smiled.

Peter moved behind her. She could feel his gaze on her bare back and silently dared him to reach out to her.

'Good morning,' he said, instead.

'Did I wake you?' she asked, turning away from the window.

'I don't think so.' He rubbed his eyes and grinned at her. 'Are you getting up?'

'Yes,' she said. 'I need to be in the city to collect my sons.'

'So, just the bed and not the breakfast, then?'

Fiona nodded. 'Sorry.'

'That's okay.' Peter's gaze wandered over her body and then slipped up to her face. 'I understand. It wasn't planned.'

'No,' Fiona said, beginning to dress. 'No, it wasn't planned.' Next time it would be though. They could mention the sex now. It would be stupid not to.

They were companionably silent as they prepared for the day. Fiona was in the bathroom tying back her hair, when Peter spoke next.

'I would like to meet your children,' he said.

Fiona saw him through the mirror. He was leaning on the door frame behind her.

'Maybe we could take them out somewhere fun?' he suggested. 'The museum perhaps? There's an Egyptian exhibit, I think.'

'They have already been, I'm afraid,' she answered. The hair elastic snapped beneath her fingers. She stayed where she was with the mirror between them.

'Somewhere else then,' Peter mused. 'We could go whale-watching. I hear they are on their way up the coast.'

'You've already met Lochie.' Fiona kept her voice firm.

Peter nodded. 'Yes, I know, but not under the best circumstances and I haven't met Hugh at all.' He smiled then, as if his expectations were reasonable ones.

Fiona stopped what she was doing and met his gaze through the glass. 'I'm afraid that won't be possible.'

'Why?'

'We have gone out a couple of times, that's all. It's not like we have begun a relationship,' she said simply, but as soon as she had, she knew nothing was simple. Peter had drawn himself up and away from the door frame. He was standing with his hands clenched at his sides, his face wooden.

'I see,' he said, nodding to himself. 'I get it.'

'What do you see?' Fiona asked because she really did want to know how he saw her before he was gone.

'You are one of those women,' he answered with authority.

'What women?'

'It is clear you've been hurt, and you are scared.'

All the time, Fiona thought.

'But the thing is, you consider all men the enemy and the only way to get over it is to get back on the horse, so to speak. Instead you don't. You put men in the position of having to prove themselves to you ...'

Absurdly, Fiona saw herself straddling him the previous evening.

'I mean, it's an impossible ask,' the doctor continued. 'How do I prove myself worthy of you? How does anybody?'

The atmosphere in the room was deformed now. Peter had begun to pace and Fiona knew if she didn't respond, he would continue to gather momentum.

'There is no need for you to prove yourself to me,' she said.

He scoffed at that. It came out as a mucous snort. 'It's what all of you women want. You want to be put on a pedestal,' he said, his anger ramping up again.

'I wanted nothing from you at all,' she said, sick of his wounds.

He stopped his pacing and grew red in the face. 'Why then, the sex? All the crotch grabbing?'

'I was drunk,' she lied.

'Maybe the first time, but not last night. You knew exactly what you were doing.'

His face was a sad mask and Fiona glimpsed who he might be when he was alone. 'I'm sorry, Peter.'

'Me too,' he said with finality. 'I'm sorry people like you are not capable of the kind of relationships which make someone feel whole.'

He left then and by the time Fiona had crossed the threshold into the bedroom, the front door was wide open and she heard his car thrum to life. She walked out onto the driveway, not to save things or say something more, but because events had overtaken her and she was stunned. Peter reversed around her like she was a tree. Then he was gone.

Back in the room, she stood beside the bed with its rumpled covers. The room felt lifeless. She gave up on it and wandered into the bathroom to collect her things. Her hairbrush lay at the edge of the sink where it didn't belong.

In the mirror, her face was pale. She tied her hair into a knot and turned away. Peter was right about some things, she knew, but he was also very wrong. Not once in her relationship with Richard had she felt whole.

✻

Steven didn't go into town. Instead he returned to his campsite and sat outside his tent with the keys to Alick's truck resting on his palm. He stared at them for a long time. It occurred to him he could leave the valley altogether. He could pack within minutes and be walking the track out to the main road. He audited his possessions: a tent, a bedroll and the army issue blanket sold cheap because of the hole, a bullet hole maybe. His fingers travelled over his pack, which he knew contained two extra shirts, two pairs of boxers, a flashlight, another pair of jeans and two pairs of shorts for warmer weather. He knew there was a knife, a razor, and a pair of cooking tongs enclosed in a sturdy pencil case so they would not pierce him through his pack. In another pencil case, not as long and squarer in shape, was a cake of soap, a comb, a condom and a roll-on deodorant.

Steven knew these items intimately because he carried them. He knew their heft. He could detect the absence of the smallest of his possessions through the pull of the pack on his shoulders and the weight of the girth strap on his hips. He wasn't like other backpackers. One day, their pack was stowed in a broom closet or the top shelf of a wardrobe, zipped closed to seal in their adventures. He had had no home to go to and had not needed one. He understood that Alick's offer shocked him. A bridge had been crossed without him meaning to cross it.

'Sven!'

Steven raised his head and heard the soft thud and swish of the boy's shoes across the grassy paddock. He pushed Alick's keys into the pocket of his jeans and stood.

'I've brought you our first egg!' Lochie called, coming into view around the curve of the hill.

The boy slowed and approached him with his hands cupped before him.

'It's only small,' Lochie said.

'Small, yes,' Steven agreed, when the egg was revealed to him. It was half the size of a supermarket egg, a deep cream with darker speckles of brown on its shell. Steven touched its cool hard shell with his finger.

'It's yours. I want you to have it for your lunch,' he said.

'Thank you, Lochie.'

Lochie transferred the egg carefully into Steven's hands. 'I have to go now, but I'll see you after school. You can tell me how it was.' Lochie made eating motions with his hands and mouth, so he might understand.

'Yes,' Steven said, nodding.

The boy ran off over the paddock through the long grass toward the farmhouse. Steven placed the egg inside his billy, surrounding it with the newspaper he used to build his fire. He looked down onto the small spotted orb nestled in its bed of paper, as the sound of the car faded into the distance. Then he placed the lid on his billy and put the container inside the entrance to his tent.

A PERFECTLY SPICED FINGERPRINT

Fiona thought she might be sick. As a contingency, she chose a seat beside a potted palm. Julia sat across from her on a matching sofa. Fiona was aware of her sister sorting through emails and her conversation with Graham over what they might eat that night. Her bile rose at the thought. Mostly, she stared through a window at the dark glossy tops of the fig trees which lined the street below and with their aid she sank below the need to know where she was.

A short woman with bandy legs entered the waiting room. She stopped and looked about her and then made a beeline for Julia and Fiona.

'Hello Fiona, my name is Lynda Hopper,' she said to Julia.

Julia shook her head, a small jerky motion, and jutted her chin toward Fiona.

'Oh, I'm sorry,' Hopper said, when she realised her mistake.

Her brown eyes oozed compassion and Fiona wondered if it were an act; that the job of family lawyering would be a sinkhole for empathy would not surprise her.

'Please, follow me,' Hopper said.

Julia was first to act with her 'let's get this over with' attitude, while Fiona trailed down the hall behind them. Without the fig trees to focus on, she felt sick again.

'So,' said Lynda. 'Let me gather some information about the present situation, so I can help. What are the children's names? How old are they?'

Fiona stared at the lawyer. The two questions threw her. How could she answer them? Lochie 12, Hugh 16, like one would in reportage, or Hugh and Lochie, 16 and 12 respectively, which sounded fit for a longer piece. She didn't know. Julia had turned in her seat to stare, urging her on. The lawyer sat calmly, non-judgmental.

'Lochie is 12 and Hugh is 16,' Julia said.

Of course, Fiona thought. That was simplest.

Hopper placed her elbows on the table and leaned toward Fiona. 'Can you tell me how long you have been separated?'

Could she tell her? It was possible she could not. 'We have been separated since January,' Fiona said, despite herself. A sigh of relief came from Julia.

'And have you decided on a property settlement?'

'No,' she said. 'I am here about the children, that's all.'

'Of course, of course. I understand,' the lawyer said.

'Should my sister be starting on a property settlement?' Julia asked.

Fiona wanted to slap her.

'Well, it's entirely up to Fiona. It's difficult to say. Every case is different. The breakdown of a marriage can be a very emotional time, so, you see, we are guided by the client.'

Fiona knew this was said for her benefit. It was Hopper's way to gain faith. 'In that case, I want you to know I don't care about the property. All I want is custody of my children.'

The lawyer nodded. 'Okay. Let's focus on that shall we. As Hugh is 16, it is his choice where he lives. The courts will be more interested in working with you and your estranged husband over Lochie's care arrangements.'

'Right,' Julia said, squeezing Fiona's hand. 'That's good, isn't it Fi?'

Fiona nodded.

'We can start proceedings to come to an agreement about joint custody. Once this has been ratified by the courts, your estranged husband cannot remove your children from you entirely without facing serious sanctions from the courts.'

Fiona stared at her. 'What do you mean, joint custody?'

'Joint custody is considered the most common arrangement these days,' Hopper replied, taking notes on a legal pad.

'Even though my sister has always been their primary carer?' Julia asked.

'Yes, even then,' the lawyer said, looking up at Julia and nodding. 'The courts consider it is in the children's best interests to have contact with both parents.'

Julia appeared to consider this idea.

Fiona stood. 'No, I can't do this,' she said, pushing her chair away so as to make her escape. The walls of the hallway leaned inward on her as she ran toward the reception area and the glass doors leading outside.

Out on the street, she took in deep breaths. Cars made their way around the small roundabout up on the corner and she watched their constant flow in and out, flaring this way and that, in an unending spiral. All those people were off to somewhere else, to homes, to businesses, to the shops, in a steady stream of intent.

'Are you all right?'

Julia was beside her again. Fiona didn't answer. She continued to watch the cars moving through the roundabout.

'Do you want to go for a walk along the river?' Julia asked.

Fiona shook her head.

'We could get a coffee then at that lovely little place just down the street,' Julia suggested.

Lochie's face came to her then, the way he had been in the car outside the produce store, wanting the best for Hugh, forgiving him too easily. She saw him again under the big tree before the dead cow day, brimming with excitement over vegetable gardens and chooks.

'It will be all right, Fi. Richard won't get the kids. I'm sure of it,' Julia said.

Fiona could tell by the way she said this she too was shocked and was trying to make the best of it. 'You don't know that,' she said.

Julia stared into the roundabout. 'I've made another appointment for this time next week, but you can change it. It seemed the right thing to do,' Julia said, her voice sounding a long way off.

Fiona looked at her sister's face in the dappled shade of the fig trees. She saw uncertainty there and it frightened her. 'I just want to go home,' Fiona said.

*

Alick stood back with his hands on his hips, surveying the cardboard boxes. He was thinking of his mother's soup tureen, the one which used to sit on the top shelf of the very same chiffonier Sven and he had hauled into his kitchen. A memory edged its way forward – white china with green vines painted on it, gold around the edges of the lid and handles and the knob on the lid at the top.

Alick hadn't thrown any of his parents' things away when he had returned from the war. He had simply packed the contents of the old farmhouse in boxes, one after another, and transferred them to his newly completed home. He'd done this in the same way he and Sven had removed the dead cow to the butchery, automatically attending to the detail. It occurred to Alick he would have packed the boxes and stacked them in the order of the rooms from which they had come.

Alick stared hard at the wall of boxes, first in the hall and then in his dining room. If he could remember which room he packed first, it would not be too difficult to locate the tureen. His mind travelled the distance between the two houses, placing the boxes. To begin at the front in one house would mean the first boxes would be stacked further in – in the sitting room rather than the hall. But he may have begun at the back of the old farmhouse which changed everything. All he needed to do was choose – front or back?

Faced with this decision, Alick baulked. He considered grabbing his rifle and seeking the solace of the paddock, of walking the fences with the sun on his shoulders. This he could do, he thought, even as he was ripping at the boxes and they were tumbling down around him like the Berlin Wall.

✻

The numbness had returned. Fiona floated like a soap bubble, looking out at a strange, strange world. As much as she tried, she could not remember dropping Julia outside her house. She must have, though. The passenger seat was empty when she pulled to a stop in the supermarket car park. This too was surprising. Her plan to shop had been made in another reality, before her lawyer's visit. Was this the madness Richard had alluded to? A trolley boy stared in at her through the windscreen of her car, his head bouncing to the beat of whatever was in his earphones. She grimaced at him and he looked away.

Fiona walked the aisles. Her method of selection was purposeless. Bread, milk, tomatoes, toothpaste, chocolate. She picked up eggs and then put them back.

'They are expensive, aren't they dear?' an elderly shopper commented.

'They are,' Fiona replied, floating on toward the cheese fridge.

She stood for a while, studying the hard and soft cheeses. Thoughts of an omelette came to her, but she would need to backtrack for the eggs, and she couldn't do that. She knew it was possible Richard could take Lochie from her.

A couple waited ahead of her in the queue to the registers, their trolley bursting with items. They too had selected tomatoes from the fresh food department, but there were also onions, zucchini, carrots and a selection of meats and sauces as accompaniments. There were his and her hair products and deodorants. This appeared in every way a routine excursion, but it was now alien to Fiona.

The woman smiled at Fiona's interest in the contents of her trolley. Fiona could not smile back. Instead, she was noticing the cleft between the woman's eyebrows. The cleft deepened and the woman turned away, busying herself with the unloading of the trolley. Hugh wouldn't go with his brother either, when he went to his father's. Lochie would be alone with Richard.

The woman's husband bent to help her. He placed the eggs beside a selection of cans and bottles.

'No, no!' the woman cried. 'The eggs go with the bread, with the bread,' she said, as if she was planning an incursion into a hostile territory and her idiot husband had forgotten to fuel the helicopter. She removed the eggs back to the trolley. 'They will break if they go in with those,' she explained, indicating the grouping of heavy objects.

'Oh,' said the man, stepping back.

She smiled at Fiona again and then at the female supermarket attendant. The young girl with her crisp, white shirt and a name badge, LEISHA, smiled conspiratorially to confirm the stupidity of cans and eggs. Fiona saw the small nod which accompanied it and the frown on a forehead not yet creased, but willing to become so.

'Men,' the woman whispered into the air and the ears of all the women grouped around the bank of cash registers. She performed this utterance as a headline with no accompanying text because it seemed none were needed.

As Fiona stepped out of the supermarket into the sunlight, she understood something had happened to her. In amongst moving to the farm, underneath the settling of their new lives and in the act of finding a small piece of space, it had slipped in unnoticed. It sat glowering now, happy as a parasite. She had failed to protect her children and she was failing still. She'd been sold a story of men and women and she'd played her part at great cost. The shame of it thudded about inside her. It pulsed in her ears, pieces of it breaking off to enter her brain. She squinted toward her car and pushed the shopping trolley across the pedestrian walkway. The pushing became progressively more difficult as if thick mud was involved. How strange, Fiona thought, as the horizon rocked and the sky faded before her. Down she went, her tomatoes arching upward and splattering on the windscreen of a smart four-wheel drive, whose driver happened to be Dr Peter Edgerton. This caused him to jerk to a stop in the belief he had killed someone, thereby narrowly missing Fiona, who lay sprawled unconscious on the pedestrian crossing.

❋

Steven ground the gearstick into a lower gear as he approached the hill. He had learned on the journey into town that the old truck could rapidly lose momentum. It could slow to a stop before the crest and Steven wanted to avoid the humiliation of rolling back down again. He gritted his teeth and planted his foot on the accelerator. The engine strained. Beside him, the box holding a new model airplane slid sideways from the seat onto the floor.

He was over the crest and coasting down the other side when he saw Fiona's children trailing along the roadside toward the farm. He knew it was her habit to drop them at the bus stop each morning and collect them in the afternoon.

The oldest boy, Hugh, walked stiffly in the lead, while Lochie trudged along behind him. Steven could see, even as he drove towards them, the gap lengthening between the two boys. He manipulated the gears again and pulled up beside Lochie. 'Do you want a ride?'

Lochie ran to the passenger door. Before he had settled in the seat beside Steven, he said, 'We don't know where Mum is.'

By the time they were on the road again, Hugh had disappeared beyond the crest of the hill. Steven jammed the truck into gear and drove after him.

When they came abreast of him, Lochie leaned out of the window. 'Sven's going to give us a lift home,' he called. 'That's good, isn't it?'

Steven could hear the uncertainty in Lochie's voice.

Hugh stopped and turned a grim face toward the utility. He frowned at Lochie, seemed about say something, then nodded and climbed in, shuffling Lochie along the bench seat until he was sitting very close to Steven. Hugh's feet tangled around the model plane. He reached down absently, picked it up and sat with the box in his lap.

Steven drove on, the three of them staring down the winding road. It started as a prickling on the back of Steven's neck. It crawled upward over the top of his head and found its way inside him. He knew this fear. He had known it all his life. Once, he had thought it normal, something everyone carried with them, but over time he realised life was easier for most. These people didn't hold back. They didn't need to hide. They inhaled with both lungs. 'We will find your mother,' he said, looking across the cabin at Lochie and Hugh. The Swedish accent was gone. This was Steven from Woodridge and he would do what he could.

'Okay,' said Lochie, just happy to find the help he needed. Hugh stared at Steven and Steven looked away again and down the road ahead.

❋

The soup tureen stood on the top shelf of the chiffonier and the wall where the boxes once rested was revealed. Alick used a tea towel to wipe the perspiration from his brow. Something close to pride washed over him. On the dining-room table sat his mother's copy of the CWA Cookbook.

The book's navy cover was worn and dusted with flour from his mother's hands. Preserved, he thought, as women like his mother liked to preserve things. Handling her things made him feel like a boy again. He could smell scones, the sweet citrus of her orange cake. He looked at his own hands. They were old now. They drew the cookbook closer and opened its cover, turning one page and then another. Alick paused over Beef & Vegetable Soup. A perfectly spiced fingerprint lay on the page.

'Alick, get out from under there and be of some use, will you? I need to get this pie baked for Sunday.'

Alick is playing under the kitchen table with his toy soldiers. One lies in some spilt gravy, having died an agonising death. Another is hunkered down behind an old envelope which has fluttered down from the table above.

'Alick!'

Alick crawls out. 'Yes, Mum?'

'Go over to the pantry and bring me the packet of arrowroot.'

Alick reaches up for the electric switch on the inside wall of the pantry. It flashes on and he is surrounded by shelves of packets and jars. The root vegetables are in a wooden box in the corner. He can smell earth. He takes his time in the pantry. He likes the small dark space. He runs his eye along the shelves, scanning for the arrowroot. He is not sure how it is spelled, but he will know the look of it when he sees it. Reading is something he is good at. He spies it on the second shelf in amongst the flours. ARROWROOT. He reaches up, takes it down and carries it to his mother.

'Thank you, Alick. You are a good boy,' she says, her attention on her mixing bowl.

He wants to ask about the arrowroot, what it's for, and whether it really is a root which looks like an arrow, but he knows better than to interrupt his mother's cooking.

Alick's hands fluttered over the recipe book before he closed it. It was a long time ago. Each summer, moving into an autumn, and onto winter and spring. Year after year. He had barely noticed the time passing, except to watch the calves be born, the steers get fat and go off to market on the back of cattle trucks.

He used the dining-room table to push himself to a standing position. His old legs groaned from sitting still too long. He was not made for sitting still. Alick pulled his gun from the rack above the front door. He had cattle to attend to.

THE JIG IS UP

The clacking of computer keys roused Fiona. She lay listening, floating on sounds. She heard murmuring and the opening and closing of doors. The clacking stopped. There was the swish of fabric and she felt the sudden pressure of fingers on her wrist. Her eyes snapped open to find a nurse leaning over her. It was the same nurse who had taken Lochie's blood a few weeks before. Her wide forehead hid the rest of the room as she focused on her wristwatch, but Fiona knew where she was. It was unfortunate, to say the least.

'I see you are awake. That's good,' she said, releasing Fiona's wrist.

'I don't remember getting here. I don't remember going to sleep at all,' Fiona said.

The nurse smiled. 'I'll let Dr Edgerton fill you in on that,' she said, handing Fiona a plastic cup of water. 'It was he who brought you in.'

Fuck. Fiona raised herself onto an elbow and took the cup. A pain ran down her arm from her shoulder.

'He won't be long,' the nurse said before leaving the room.

Fiona inspected her shoulder with the tips of her fingers. The muscle was hot to touch.

'You will be sore, but it's only bruising.' Peter stood in the doorway, just as he had at the B&B, but his face was a mask and he was stranger.

'What happened?' Fiona asked.

'You fell hard on the road,' he said. 'In front of my car, in fact.' His words were clipped, his responses precise and professional.

'Did I knock myself out?' she asked him, ignoring his coldness.

Peter took a wide berth around her and sat at his desk. 'Either that or you fainted first,' he sighed.

She could tell he preferred his second theory – women who fainted. Fiona drew herself up to a sitting position despite the pain in her shoulder. 'How long have I been here? My children will be worried.'

'About an hour and a half.'

'Well, thank you for helping me, Peter.'

Peter sniffed and opened his prescription pad. 'I'll give you an anti-inflammatory and you can take paracetamol to help with the pain. Other than that, you should need no further medical advice.'

Fiona stared at the top of his head as he bent over his prescription pad. 'I'm sorry about the other morning,' she said, quietly.

'Your bag and groceries are behind reception and your car is outside,' was his only response.

'Right,' she said, slipping off the exam table to collect the prescription.

Out in the waiting room, Fiona pulled out her phone. The screen was badly cracked, but still responsive. There was a missed call from Renee Rodgers, but she could deal with that later, five calls from Hugh's phone and another three from the farmhouse. She dialled the house.

Hugh answered. 'Where were you? Why didn't you answer?'

Fiona heard the panic in his voice and she knew he had been thinking of Richard. 'It's all right, Hugh. I fell over in the supermarket car park. That's all. How did you get home?'

'Sven drove by and picked us up.'

Fiona could hear him closing off now the threat was over. 'Thank him for me, won't you?'

'You should have rung me,' Hugh insisted.

'Yes, I know. I'm coming home now.'

✳

The muscles across Steven's shoulders ached with effort. He imagined them as thick, pink elastic bands like those used to bundle mail, drawing taut and relaxing from his neck to the upper joint of his arm. He would not dwell on his mistake. The rhythm of the axe would shut it out.

Three times that morning he drove the paddocks along the treeline, threw the timber into the tray of the utility, and returned to split and chop the wood. The space under the awning was almost full. He had learnt to let the heavy axe do the work, taking the strain of its heft skywards and guiding it on the way down.

Three large pieces remained to be split, when he sensed a presence behind him. Steven relaxed his shoulders and turned. Hugh stood a short distance off, scowling. Steven nodded in acknowledgement and returned to his labour.

Even with his back turned, he felt Hugh's anger. It had a silent volume of its own. It vibrated across his shoulders where the muscle laid, the pink rubber bands pulled too tight now. Steven leant the axe against the chopping block and lifted another log. He centred it and hoisted the axe again. The splinters flew and the log cracked, once, twice and again, until it was divided into four. He walked the segments to the pile and placed them. Hugh remained where he was, beyond the flight of splinters. Steven chose another log.

'You are not who you say you are,' the boy said.

Steven paused bent over his chopping block. He felt the thick coating of bark under his hand and he saw the smoothness of the wood beneath. He knew everything had changed and he would be moving on.

'Who is?' he said to the log, as he positioned it. The axe curved high and fell. The cut was deep. Steven swung again. The wood sliced open, the trauma irreversible.

The boy stepped forward. Hugh placed the wedges of wood in the cradle of his arm and transferred them to the pile. He positioned another log on the block for Steven.

❋

Fiona pushed two pain killers from the foil packet and swallowed them without water. She was back in the waiting room at Fair Work Nation. At the eleventh hour, Renee Rodgers had come through with a name of a bullying victim who was willing to talk.

A buzzer sounded and the receptionist reached for the telephone. 'Yes, I'll escort her in,' she said.

Fiona was ushered down the hall to the same meeting room she had visited two weeks earlier. A tall young woman in a stylish suit rose from her chair beside Renee. 'Hello, I'm Leanne Ferguson,' she said, leaning over the table to shake hands. 'I hope you don't mind if I have Renee stay during the interview.'

The young woman spoke rapidly, her words almost clipped in two before they were out of her mouth, and Fiona knew she was nervous. 'Not at all,' she answered, taking her seat. 'May I call you Leanne?'

The woman nodded once, a quick jerk of her head.

'So, Leanne, can you tell me what caused you to contact Fair Work Nation?'

Leanne inhaled deeply. She nodded once to herself, a single jerk of her head again, reminding Fiona of her sister. Then, she clasped her hands in front of her and spoke more slowly this time. 'From the moment I started working at Wallis Industries, other members of the management team and, in some cases, my subordinates made my job difficult,' she replied.

'In what way?'

'Well, to begin with, I was not invited to meetings where my input would have been valuable.'

'Can you give me an example?'

'Sure. Quarterly planning meetings, where the quantities of product and dates for shipments were discussed,' Leanne explained. 'I was employed in a management position on the back of my experience in logistics and South East Asian affairs,' she explained. 'Wallis Industries transports their plastics all over the country and was beginning to export into South Korea and Thailand.'

'I see. How did you respond to being excluded?'

'I asked for a meeting with Gene Pickering and the vice-president, Jeremy Cox, to reconfirm my job description. I thought maybe there had been a misunderstanding regarding my role.'

'And was there?' Fiona asked.

'That was difficult to ascertain,' Leanne said.

'Why?'

'Neither Pickering nor Cox agreed to meet with me.'

'What, never?' Fiona had not expected this.

'That's right,' Leanne was emphatic.

Fiona glanced over at Renee who, until this point had been sitting quietly by in support.

Now she interjected. 'I know this is not what people expect to hear when an accusation of bullying is made, but this kind of behaviour is every bit as common as stand-over tactics and threats, Fiona. Particularly, when the bullying is occurring higher up in the hierarchy.'

'Really?'

'Oh yes, the complete story of bullying has not been told. It's a bit like the assumption that women secretly enjoy being sexually harassed and domestic violence only occurs in lower socio-economic groups.'

Fiona stared at Renee, but the advocate had already turned to Leanne and was patting her on the shoulder. Fiona cleared her throat and refocused on Leanne. 'So, what was going on, in your opinion?'

Leanne Ferguson arched an eyebrow at Fiona. 'In my opinion, I wasn't Pickering's or Cox's first choice for the position. My recommendation had come via a colleague in Thailand, a powerful colleague they needed to impress. I believe Cox and Pickering were setting me up to fail.'

'How?'

Leanne looked to Renee and the advocate smiled reassuringly.

'I was not given access to the information I needed to do my job. Of course, I didn't know this right away. It was only when I was invited to address the board on the effectiveness of my strategy for exports to Thailand and South Korea and my progress to date, that I realised how screwed I was. The truth was I had no strategy. I was given no information with which to formulate one.'

'Right. That's tough. So, what did you do?'

'I stormed into Pickering's office and yelled at lot. He did a reasonable job of pretending he didn't know what I was talking about and asked me why, if I was having problems, didn't I contact him sooner?'

'God, you must have hit the roof,' Fiona gasped.

'I did and that is when he and Cox called security and had me removed from the building. I was told to go home and cool down. Instead, I came in here and lodged my complaint.'

Fiona nodded encouragingly.

'From then on, until I landed my new job, I was treated as unstable by almost all of the staff. I was still not included in meetings, but now it seemed they had good reason. I was a crazy cow. As you can imagine, I was unable to present a report to the board due to a lack of anything to report and was given a warning that I was in breach of my work contract.' Leanne stopped abruptly and stared again at her hands. When she spoke next, her voice trembled. 'The fact that I couldn't do my job made me feel so ashamed.'

Fiona reached out and squeezed her hands. 'I'm so sorry, Leanne. What did you do then?'

'I did the only thing I could think of. I started applying for jobs. In a month, I was appointed manager of logistics for a South Korean firm. I dropped the case, left all of it behind me and moved to Seoul. But that month was just awful, you know? When people treat you like a failure, you start making mistakes and pretty soon you feel like it's all your fault. If I hadn't experienced some success prior to my job at Wallis's, this might have ruined me. It almost did.'

＊

Alick fell into a deep sleep while his soup bubbled away. As he drifted off in his broken recliner with his feet higher than they ought to be, he reconsidered his father's chair in the storage shed. He might ask Sven to bring it in after all.

Nearly an hour later, he was woken by the telephone. 'What?' His voice was thick with sleep.

'Is that you, Alick? Are you all right?' Harry asked.

Alick readjusted himself in his chair. 'I'm fine. What do you want?'

'Well, I was just at Sweeney's. They are about to close up and are wondering why your truck is still parked outside.'

'What? My truck?' Alick felt a knot of anxiety slither and tighten.

'Yep. They say the lad brought it in earlier,' Harry said. 'It's been there since midday, and the keys are in it.'

'Right ...' Alick said. 'Just give me half an hour, would you?'

'Okay, I'll hang about for a bit then,' Harry said.

The smell of beef and vegetable soup filled his nostrils. Alick pushed himself to his feet and turned off the hotplate. He took his gun down from the shelf above the door and set off for Sven's campsite.

He came upon it before he meant to. A square of dead grass and the lifeless cooking fire was all that remained. Alick sat on a stump in front of the cold ashes. Before him was the grassy rise, the green of that grass against the blue of the sky. This had been home to the boy. He nodded to himself. It wasn't a bad home. Cooler now, the seasons had changed, but hunkered down in behind the small rise and, with the ridge at his back, the lad would have been okay.

Alick looked down at the fire and prodded it with a stick. He had overstepped. If he hadn't offered him a room in the house, the lad would be here still. He was sure of it. He sat for a long time until his bones began to ache. Finally, he dug the butt of his rifle into the earth and raised himself to his feet.

'It seems the boy has moved on,' Alick said when he returned Harry's call.

'Okay, I'm sorry about that Alick. Don't you worry about the truck. Sweeney and I will get it back to you, quick-smart.'

Alick walked up the stairs to the second bedroom and looked in. He'd rearranged the bed to get more light from the window and beside it he had placed the green leather-topped side-table he had found in the shed.

Daisy lowed from the house paddock below the window, a reminder that it was milking time.

❋

Steven watched the streetlights, car lights, and floodlit car parks roll by the train window, washes and streaks of colour in the darkness. The fields and farm fences were behind him now and in his mind they would fade too. The valley would become one of the many places he once worked, no better, no worse. He had shaken off the stupor of the farm, shocked out of it by Hugh.

He rubbed the callouses on his palm with a thumb. It was comforting. He drew the backpack closer and slid down in his seat. The lights behind the window tilted. Now he saw only the streetlights above him.

Sleep didn't come though, Alick did, with his old face, crinkled and worn. Harry, too, in his big four-wheel drive.

He saw Fiona. He imagined them around the dinner table in the old farmhouse – Lochie and Hugh talking and talking, as if this was the most natural thing in the world to do. He saw Daisy, the big globes of her eyes. He heard the milk squirting into the aluminium pail. For the rest of his life, he would know that sound. He drifted for a long time in Daisy's eyes, the train slowing at stations, stopping and then moving on. He hadn't known he liked animals.

COOKING SOUP

Fiona had been working on the Leanne Ferguson story all afternoon. She and Steph had agreed on two distinct stories – one which reflected workplace culture, bullying legislation and statistics, and the other, a profile of Leanne's experiences at Wallis Industries. It was starting to come together. All she needed to do was focus on the emotional cost to the victim. She rewound the tape, watching the counter. It was important to get the sequence right in her head. Fiona stopped the recorder and pressed play. '... fact that I couldn't do my job made me feel so ashamed.' Fiona stopped the tape and recorded the time. It was very close to her best quote, except for '... pretty soon you feel like it's all your fault.' She had already marked that. Fiona rewound the tape further and Renee Rodgers' voice came through clearly. 'It's a bit like the assumption that women secretly enjoy being sexually harassed and –' Fiona pressed the stop button. She knew what came next and fast-forwarded again. '... I was treated as unstable.' And again. '... I was a crazy cow.' And then. '... you start making mistakes.' She could hear her

154

pulse in her ears. It was as if Leanne Ferguson had climbed inside her head. She rewound the tape to find just the right place. She closed her eyes and listened. 'Oh yes,' Renee Rodgers said, 'the complete story of bullying has not been told. It's a bit like the assumption that women secretly enjoy being sexually harassed and domestic violence only occurs in lower socio-economic groups.'

Fiona pushed herself away from the table. Fuck. The wrench on her sore shoulder brought tears to her eyes. Slowly, she rotated the joint as she walked down the hall. Before a small mirror, she undid the top buttons of her shirt and examined her shoulder in the bathroom mirror. It had been a week since her fall in the supermarket car park. Dark blues and purples against white skin, a pretty palette elsewhere. She rotated the joint again and winced. Not broken, though. That she knew.

She is unpacking boxes, reaching over her pregnant belly to bring out item after item. The photographs from university in their plastic frames look cheap and they don't belong. She places the papier-mâché bowl she made when pregnant with Hugh in the middle of the table. It looks a poor thing in the cavernous room, as does the table, the chairs and herself. She hates the house. It is not them, but then she is no longer sure there is a them. Richard's success has changed him. He is less kind. She crosses to the double doors which look out over the backyard. The house is positioned high, her line of sight above the back fence. Tall trees mask the yards of their new neighbours. We have been elevated, she thinks.

She hears Richard swear his way through the front door. Really, he is happy. Happier than he has ever been, imagining the entertaining they will do to further his career. He no longer talks of hers. He makes his way into the combined kitchen and sitting room where she is.

'How are you going?' he asks, impatient with the number of boxes still left unpacked.

'I'll get it done. It's been a long day, that's all.' She rubs her back, which aches all the time now the baby is almost due.

Richard crosses to the doors and stands beside her looking out. 'It's wonderful, isn't it?'

'Yes,' she says, but something inside her sniffs with sadness.

He studies her then. 'You don't think it's great?' he asks.

'Yes,' she says, nodding. 'It is. It's just that I miss our old place too, you know? It was our first home together and it was where Hugh was born.'

Half of the way through this sentence Fiona knows something is wrong. She feels a drop in air pressure, but before she can decipher him, she feels the sting of a slap across her face.

'That place was a dump, you know. I couldn't wait to leave it behind,' Richard says, his shoulders squared toward the glass doors.

'How dare you,' Fiona cries, raising a hand to push him away from her.

Richard grabs her hand. 'You want to fight me? Do you? Then fight!' He pushes her balled fist hard against the solid wooden door frame and she hears the bone crack. The pain is beyond noise and she grasps her hand, too frightened to look at it.

'It's broken,' she says, as if to herself.

Richard stalks out of the room. 'Don't be stupid,' he calls to her.

Fiona hears Hugh crying from his room down the hall. She hurries to him and picks him up. A shaft of pain travels from her damaged hand up her shoulder.

Richard reappears in the doorway. He watches as she fumbles with Hugh. 'Fuck, Fi. You're such a klutz.' His voice has changed. It's softer now. 'Come on,' he says quietly. 'Let's get that hand seen to.'

A chill runs through Fiona. It is as if it had nothing to do with him.

'Kickboxer?' the doctor says, smiling.

'No,' she says. 'Why?' She asks only to divert herself. Everything feels unreal.

'Most common injury in boxing,' he says, gently manipulating the small bones in her hand. 'Not usually a sport enjoyed by heavily pregnant women, though.'

'No,' she says. Richard has left the room with Hugh on his hip to return the paperwork to the front desk.

The doctor waits for her to speak.

It is so recent in her mind, she cannot.

'Is there something wrong?'

Fiona looks into his kind brown eyes. Everything, she thinks. Nothing could be the same now. 'No, no. I'm a klutz, that's all. I was unpacking boxes in our new house and I lost my balance.'

The doctor nods as if this makes perfect sense.

'Mummm – it's Grandma on the phone!'
Lochie's voice pulled at her. Fiona fastened the buttons on her shirt to hide the bruise. 'I'm coming.'

She took the phone from Lochie's outstretched hand. 'Hello, Mum.'

'How are you? We haven't heard from you for a while. Your father and I have been worried.'

'I'm fine,' Fiona said, rotating her shoulder. 'How are you and Dad?'

'Oh, you know. The same. Your father has found a better butcher. The meat isn't quite as good as the farmer's, though.'

Her mother's favourable mention of Alick and the cow surprised her. 'I hope it was fresh.'

'Indeed, it was,' Gwendolyn said.

Fiona walked through the house and took up her favourite chair on the verandah. She looked toward the large tree. In her mind's eye, the cow twirled in the air. 'So, where is this new butcher? I'm coming into town for a conference soon and maybe I can pick up some meat.'

'You know the Caltex service station? It's down a bit behind Rosie's Chocolate Shop,' Gwendolyn said.

'Right. I'll check it out.'

A silence stretched between them. Fiona looked down the track toward the creek. The sound of cars far off on the main road made her think of the doctor and the B&B. Already, it seemed long ago. How strange, she thought.

She heard her mother take a deep breath.

'Is everything okay, Mum?'

When Gwendolyn's voice came, it was uncertain. 'Julia told me about your visit to the lawyer's office.'

'I'm sorry, Mum. I know I should have told you about it.'

'I suppose you and Richard are divorcing, then,' she said flatly.

'We are sorting out custody of the children first,' Fiona said. Her mouth was dry, and she swallowed hard. She had thought she had more time to work out how to tell them. Damn, Julia.

'Fiona, I don't understand. Why would you need a custody arrangement?'

'Mum, it's just better to have it in writing, that's all.'

'I see,' Gwendolyn said, as if she didn't see at all.

'Don't worry, Mum. Everything will work out.'

'You are telling me your marriage is over, then?'

'Yes, Mum. My marriage is over.'

Gwendolyn let out a long sigh. 'I just don't understand.'

Fiona heard the dismay in her mother's voice.

'I mean, I'm finding it hard to imagine you and Richard not being together. It's always been that way.'

Fiona felt this in her heart. Of all the people to explain her own sadness and failure, it was her mother. 'I know, Mum, but sometimes things don't work ...'

'But that's it, isn't it? You fix what doesn't work. That's what people do.' Gwendolyn made her appeal. 'That's what your father and I do!'

'Look, Mum, I've got to go. Can we talk about this later?'

'Okay, but, Fiona – I need you to give this a try, if not for you and Richard, for the children.'

＊

Alick was bent over the wire strainers, ratcheting up the tension until the wire thrummed when he plucked it with his thumb. He paused and cocked his head just long enough to recognise the sound of Harry's four-wheel drive. He had half expected him the day before, but it was the Sweeney boys who brought the truck back.

He tied off the wire and released the strainers as Harry drove around the side of the shed. The door opened wide and the vet slid to the ground and headed straight for him.

'How's it going, old man?' he said, pushing his hat to the back of his head.

Alick grunted.

'Good, then?' Harry said.

'It's the same, I'd say,' Alick replied.

'Not quite the same, though is it?' Harry said, as he followed Alick to the shed. Alick disappeared into the darkness and returned the wire strainers to their place on the wall. It was going to be one of those conversations. They happened rarely and were never welcome. He could see Harry's outline as the vet waited for him in the light. The vet's paunch had grown substantially, bulging over the belt of his trousers. Pub meals, Alick thought.

Harry peered into the shadowy recesses of the barn, his eyes flicking here and there, as if what he sought eluded him. Alick found the play-acting annoying.

'So, Sven's really gone then?' he asked.

'Yep, he's gone. Had to happen sometime.'

'Why?' Harry asked.

'Sven's a traveller.'

'Still,' Harry said, 'he struck me as someone who would stay for a bit.'

Maybe Alick had felt the same thing and this was why he had offered the lad a room. 'Wouldn't be the first time you've been wrong, Harry.'

The vet wedged a foot into the wheel arch of the tractor and leant on his bent knee. 'No, I guess not. Shame though, isn't it?' Harry stared at Alick.

The old farmer kept his face impassive. 'Want a cuppa?' he said instead.

'Sure thing.'

Harry took a chair at the dining-room table as Alick boiled the jug. 'That's a damn nice soup tureen, Alick. I don't think I noticed it before.'

'It was my mother's,' Alick said. He knew what was coming and was rethinking his decision about offering Harry tea.

'My God, man. You've unpacked the boxes?'

And there it was. He was in hell.

'What made you do it after all this time?'

Alick carried in the mugs and two biscuits on a plate. 'I needed some things,' he said.

'What things?' Harry asked, swivelling his head this way and that to take in the room.

'Cooking things,' Alick answered.

'What are you cooking then?'

'Christ, man. I'm cooking soup, if that's okay with you!'

❁

Fiona's phone rang through the car's speaker system.

'Are you going?' Julia asked straight off.

'Yes, I'm on my way there now.'

Julia sighed into the phone. 'Good. That's good. Do you want me to come? I could be with you in half an hour?'

'No, it's alright, Jules,' Fiona replied. She had questions she couldn't ask the lawyer in front of Julia. Fiona changed lanes on the freeway to avoid a slow-moving truck.

'Okay, then.' Julia sounded disappointed.

'Mum rang,' Fiona said.

'She did?'

Fiona heard stress in her voice. 'Yes. She wanted to know why we went to see a lawyer.'

'I'm sorry, Fi. I know I shouldn't have told her. It's just that she asks all the time and I suppose I thought it was a positive thing ... It is a positive thing.'

'I don't think Mum sees it that way,' Fiona said.

'No.'

Fiona could almost feel her sister thinking.

'She'll come around, Fi. She's just not good with change, that's all. You've got to admit it's going to take a bit for all of us. Richard has always been there.'

Fiona hit the brakes when she saw a police car in her rear-view mirror. 'Fuck!'

'What?' Julia yelled back.

The police car took an exit ramp and Fiona exhaled with relief. 'Police car,' she said.

'Slow down, Fiona, for god's sake!'

'I am!'

Julia said nothing.

'Jules?' Fiona tried to fish her sister out of the dead air.

'Fiona, it's not important. Really, it's not,' Julia said.

'What isn't?'

'Look, I get it. It's more complicated than it was in Mum's day. I know. I feel it too, but I don't get why you never talk about it or why the kids don't see Richard. I really don't. It's strange. You've ...'

Fiona knew her sister was looking around for the right word.

'You've changed,' she said finally.

A silence opened up between them. A yawning, gaping void. Fiona pulled into the car park outside the lawyer's offices. She sat gripping the wheel. Everything had changed. How could she explain it?

'Fi?' Julia's voice was small and afraid.

'He hit me, Julia. He broke bones and I can't fix that.'

It was out now.

❋

Lynda Hopper sat at the conference table with a leather binder in front of her. A glass of water stood at her elbow and another was placed where Fiona would sit. A box of tissues sat discreetly on the sideboard.

'Good morning,' she said, as Fiona sat and pulled a notebook from her bag.

Fiona nodded.

'I see your sister is not with you. I hope she is well.'

There was softness around her cheeks, the clear forehead, the head craned forward just a little, waiting for an answer. The best Fiona could come up with was a kind of unintended, muted pleasantness. 'She is well, thank you, and I am sorry to have ended our last meeting the way I did'.

Hopper didn't acknowledge the apology. 'Is it possible you want to speak to me without your sister present?'

Once again, the neck craned forward in anticipation. The eyes were direct now.

'Yes,' Fiona replied.

The lawyer nodded and looked pointedly at Fiona's notebook.

'Right,' Fiona said, opening the notebook and cleared her throat. The questions she had written were indecipherable now. She had planned to lead up to her most pressing question, but out it came. 'Under what circumstances would a parent be granted full custody over their children?'

'I see. Well, it's becoming less common, but I know from experience, if the other parent has been involved in a serious criminal act – paedophilia comes to mind or murder – or where neglect or abuse of the children can be proven, it is often the case that the courts will award custody to the other parent. If there is serious mental illness, which would prevent a parent carrying out their parental responsibilities, the court would consider sole custody or monitored visits.' Hopper's expression remained impassive.

'I understand,' Fiona said.

The lawyer leaned over the table again, as if she were sharing sensitive material. Fiona watched for this behaviour in interviews. It either meant she was a whistle-blower of some sort, or she was lying.

'Of course, if there has been family violence and the police are aware of the situation, the court would consider joint custody not in the best interests of the children.' The lawyer paused and studied Fiona carefully. 'Might this be the case with you and your children, Fiona?'

Fiona looked down at the table. Whistle-blower.

Lynda sighed. 'Look, I've worked in family law for twenty years. I've seen a lot. Can I ask you if the police are aware of the violence?'

Fiona shook her head.

'Doctors or hospital staff?'

'No,' Fiona said.

'Are you currently in danger, Fiona?'

Fiona felt pressure on her chest and her shoulder began to ache again. 'He doesn't know where we are.'

'Has there been any violence or threats in the last six months?'

'No. I've been gone for six months. Why?'

'Well, it's harder to get a restraining order, if there have been no recent incidents.'

'I don't need a restraining order,' Fiona snapped. The thought of it made Fiona feel unwell.

Hopper held up her hands. 'All right, there is another matter to consider. Now, I know you don't want to begin negotiating a property settlement, but you might want to consider getting this over as soon as possible, so you can start fresh. I know it's hard to imagine a world where you have moved on from all of this, but I want you to try,' she said. 'There is so much you could do with a new life.'

'I'm not ready,' Fiona said.

'Just think about it. That's all I'm saying.'

Fiona looked out of the window down onto the street. People walked along the footpaths. Some crossed the street in between the traffic. The lawyer made some notes in her folder. The scratching of the cheap biro came to Fiona like a radio not quite on station. She kept her eyes on the people in the street.

'Fiona?'

'Yes?' Lynda Hopper was studying her, perhaps she had been doing so for some time.

'Does your sister know about the violence?' Lynda asked.

'Yes.'

'How long has she known?'

'About an hour, I think.'

'I see.'

✳

It was dark when Steven found himself outside his old house. He hadn't meant to ever return. His legs had taken him to the platform for the all-stops to Beenleigh train. He'd sat with the other passengers, watching the lights come on in passing homes, lurching forward with each stop. He felt there was something mechanical about all of them, himself included.

A 'TO RENT' sign stood in the front yard of the house. Someone had drawn a moustache on the estate agent's face and had scrawled FUCKER across it like a tattoo. In another neighbourhood, this would have been sorted quickly, but no one had come to replace the sign. It would, like every other eyesore, become part of the landscape.

Steven skirted the property, keeping to the shadows cast by the fence. Nothing had changed. The fence still teetered inwards on dodgy posts. The old clothesline was still missing one of its plastic-coated wires from the time one of his mother's boyfriends had wrapped it around her neck. The back stairs were still missing the first step.

He stood wondering. If so little had changed, it just might be there. He picked up the stone which lay to one side of the stairs. The hollow where a key once lay was bare. Steven carried the stone up the stairs and broke the window in the back door. He used his jacket to protect himself from the glass shards and opened the door from the inside.

No lights came on when he flicked the switch, but there was enough light from the street to bring out the shape of the old lounge. He knew it. Orange with grime-coloured armrests. His memory laid the ghost of his mother on it. Her arm rested on her brow with her elbow outflung. One knee was bent against the back rest, her head lolled as it did when she was high. Steven turned away. Apart from the sofa, there was no other furniture in the house. Steven slipped past the bathroom because he knew he would see her there too.

It took no time at all for him to unpack his hiking mat and sleeping bag. The water flowed from the faucet in the kitchen into his kettle and he ignited the old gas cooker with a match. Steven sat on the floor, watching the blue ring of the gas fire flicker. There was a need to silence the kettle before it sang.

A BOY'S TEARS

Fiona lay awake at 3am. She had already counted the wood panels across the ceiling of her bedroom. Then she counted the panels on each wall and discovered she lived in a perfect cube. Each time her mind drifted to the conversation with her lawyer, she drew it away again and recounted.

She found her slippers by the light of her reading lamp and crept down the hall into the kitchen. The air was cold and thin in the way it was far from the benign winds of the coast. She warmed her hands on the kettle as it boiled. Through the kitchen window the world was black. No streetlights. No other lights of any kind. Gradually, she had grown used to it. She liked it, even. She could pull the darkness around herself.

Fiona sat on the sofa in front of her laptop and drew it toward her. The conference was coming and there was backgrounding to do. She would talk with Gordon Watts again for the sexual harassment story. They had planned that already, but she needed to sniff about for other story ideas too. She browsed through the program and made a note of the presentations which might be interesting, but fatigue crept up on her. When her tea was finished, she placed the laptop on the coffee table and laid down on the sofa.

Before dawn, Fiona was roused by a shriek. An echo of it was all that was left by the time she was fully awake. She waited and then she heard it again and then again, accompanied by flapping and squawking. She jammed her feet back into her slippers, grabbed a torch from the kitchen and ran out of the back door and around the side of the house. A reddish lump of feathers lay at the open door to the chicken pen. Squawking came from the small enclosure. She shone her light inside and saw a flash of red eyes and a cruel smile curled around a half-dead chicken. The fox turned to face her, still now and staring. The blood pumped into her head and she knew hate. The chicken in its jaws appeared weaker. Blood trickled and dropped to the dirt. 'You bastard,' she whispered.

Fiona stood as still as possible. To move would break the spell and the fox would be gone. At the very periphery of her vision was Hugh's shovel. He had left it leaning against the long side of the chicken run. She snaked her hand out toward it, not breaking her gaze with the fox, as if in doing so the fox would be fooled. He was not. Fiona saw the change in him. The creature made a leap for the doorway and snaked between her legs to freedom. Fiona threw the shovel with everything she had. Like a javelin, it soared and then dipped. It came down as the fox ran under the barbed wire and into the paddock. With the fence between them, it stopped, looking back to leer at her, but it was wrong to do so. The shovel came down blade first. It struck the creature on its back, tilted and then flipped away. It clattered onto the ground. By the dim dawn light, she saw it falter and fall. Its legs crumpled beneath it and, despite its struggles, they did not move again. The fox watched her. Its lips were drawn back. Short panting breaths rocked its body. Fiona's lips were drawn back too. Likewise, she panted, but not from pain, but from a deep and unfathomable dismay. She flinched when she heard the gunshot. The fox shuddered. Its eyes grew wide before it rolled over and lay still.

She looked to the ridge, as the farmer bought the gun down to his side. Her own shock kicked her legs out from under her and she sat down heavily in the yard next to the dead chickens. Lochie and Hugh rushed out of the house. Lochie began to howl and Hugh walked into the paddock towards the dead fox.

❊

The dawn bathed the scene in cheery light. It shone off the shovel blade in the paddock grass. Alick frowned. He, of all people, was familiar with the variables in play. Wind, temperature, humidity, light, heft, weapon and, in this case, strength, but he also knew what rage could do. Foxes made you hate them. They were cruel animals, over-equipped to kill chickens. He had seen their carnage as a child. The blood, the feathers, the birds' bodies exposed for the flimsy creatures they were.

The older boy leaned closer to the dead fox and Alick knew he was searching for the bullet hole. 'In the ear,' the old man muttered to himself.

The little boy's sobs floated to him. Alick shouldered his gun and set off down the paddock. He came abreast of Hugh, who was poking the body of the dead fox with the shovel. He paused and grunted. 'Your mother broke his back with that.' The boy's eyes widened.

Alick stood on the lowest string of the barbed-wire fence and manoeuvred through the gap. Lochie looked to him, cradling one of the dead chickens. The farmer patted him on the shoulder. 'It will be all right, boy.'

Fiona struggled to her feet. 'It's dead,' she said, her voice far away.

Alick could see the shock in her eyes. 'Yes, it's dead.'

'Yes,' she said, nodding.

'We need to bury those chickens,' Alick said. He motioned to Hugh beyond the fence to bring the shovel.

Fiona nodded. 'Thank you. We should get the fox too, I suppose?'

'No, no. We don't bury the fox,' he said. 'We hang it from the fence as a warning to its kind.'

Fiona stared at him but said nothing.

Hugh bought the shovel. Alick indicated the wheelbarrow by the vegetable garden and the boy retrieved it. The farmer lifted the first body and placed it in the barrow. Lochie lifted the next, while Hugh stood by with the shovel. When all six of the dead chickens were collected, Alick turned to Lochie. 'Where would you like to bury them?'

Lochie looked around in the yard. 'There,' he said, pointing towards the shade beneath the pepper tree. A tear traced its way down his cheek.

'That is a fine place,' Alick said.

While Hugh's shovel was biting into the dark, rich soil, Fiona stood looking out into the paddock toward the fox. 'I need the wheelbarrow,' she said. One by one, she lifted the dead chickens, until a line of bodies lay nestled into each other. She turned the empty barrow toward the paddock.

'I can do that,' said Alick.

Fiona shook her head. 'Could you help me through the fence though?'

He stood on the bottom wire and raised the middle strand for Fiona to push the barrow through. Alick followed.

She paused and inhaled sharply, as Alick knew she would. It was shocking how easily life could be taken. He raised the body by the tail and laid it in the wheelbarrow.

'I wanted to kill it,' she said, quietly.

'Yes,' he said.

She stood very still. Alick could not hear her breathing.

'Can you teach me how to shoot?' she asked.

'Shoot?'

'Yes.' She looked toward the rifle in his hand.

'No,' Alick said, turning the wheelbarrow toward the fence line.

'Why?' she asked.

Alick paused. 'Because it won't do you any good.'

They stood side by side for a while, staring at the fox in the wheelbarrow.

'Sven has gone,' Alick said.

'He's gone?' Fiona asked.

'Yes,' said Alick.

*

The matted fur of the fox's tail stirred in the breeze. It was rich and lush. Once, Fiona might be encouraged to run a hand through it, but now she was without pity. She took a sip of her coffee, as Hugh came out of the house.

'Hi,' he said, perching on the verandah railing.

'Hey,' she said.

He watched her drink her coffee and said nothing. Fiona could almost imagine herself alone.

'You nearly killed it,' he said, pointing to the body in the fence wire.

'Yes,' she said.

'Do you feel bad?' he asked.

'No,' she said. It was the truth.

Hugh nodded. He looked back toward the fox.

He could hate her, Fiona thought. Let him do that. There was little she could do about it.

Hugh slipped off the rail and took up the seat beside her. 'Have you fixed things with Dad?'

'Nope,' she said.

'I hate him,' he said. Fiona took her eyes from the dead fox. He cried then in a way he hadn't done since he was small. She felt all of his fear and his misery seep out of him into the air around them.

'I know you do,' she said. She should never have pretended otherwise. She laid an arm across his shoulders. 'I don't want you involved, Hugh. It's not up to you,' she said.

'I know. I'm sorry.'

Fiona let the apology wash over her. She sat with her arm across Hugh's shoulders as his crying slowed. She knew there was distance between them. There would always be now. It was the space which existed between one person and another and one she would learn to respect. Hugh straightened in his seat, his tears gone.

She took another sip of her coffee. 'Did you know that Sven has left?'

'No,' Hugh said.

'Alick told me.'

Hugh cleared this throat and squirmed in his chair.

'What?' Fiona asked.

Hugh stared down at the old wooden planks on the verandah. He pushed the toe of his runner against an uneven board. 'I don't think he is Swedish.'

'What do you mean?'

'I think he's Australian.'

'Why?'

Hugh turned to her. 'You know the afternoon when you fell over in town and he picked us up?'

'Yes.'

'We were really worried, and he told us that he would help us find you, except he didn't have an accent then.'

'Really?' Fiona searched Hugh's face for the truth.

'Yep.'

'Did you ask him about it?'

'I told him that I didn't believe he was who he said he was, and he said, 'Who is?''

'So, he didn't deny it?'

'No.'

Hugh and Fiona sat for a long time staring out at the dead fox. In the time since they had last liked each other, Hugh had changed. So had she.

*

Steven left the local supermarket with a cheap cooler bag, some frozen peas, and some sausages for his dinner. He would use the gas stove in the old kitchen and his foldaway skillet to complete the task.

'Stevie, man! Is that Stevie boy?'

Steven stiffened. Across the street, Boner was leaning up against a tall paling fence smoking a cigarette. Boner Philips had been the dumbest boy in tenth grade at Woodridge North Secondary. It was undisputed by fellow students, teachers and Boner's own parents. Steven had not seen him for five years. 'Hey, Boner,' he said, as if it was only yesterday. The neighbourhood etiquette had returned to Steven with the exhaust fumes, diamond-wire fences, and howling babies.

'Hey, man,' said Boner, crossing the street to join him. 'Long time, no see.' Boner never had played it cool. 'Where did you take off to? I went to your mum's funeral, so we could catch up. The social service people were there asking if there was a kid, but we never speak to them arseholes, you know.'

'Thanks. I had to get out before they threw me into foster care.'

Boner nodded. Everybody in the neighbourhood knew the system. He changed his weight from one leg to the other and dug into his pocket. 'Do you want a durrie?' He pulled out a flattened packet of cigarettes and waggled it at Steven.

'Nah, man, but thanks.'

'Have you seen Marius yet?' Boner asked.

Steven shook his head. Marius was considered his older cousin. Their mothers were friends, both Swedish, both drug-fucked.

'Maybe, you should. He's top-shit around here. Knows everybody. Keeps the peace.'

Steven nodded. He realised he wasn't all that surprised. Marius had been a benign hoodlum. 'I might drop by his place,' he said. 'Is he still at his Mum's on Wagner Street?'

'Sure is,' Boner said. He seemed intent on scoping down the road a way.

'Are you waiting for someone?' Steven asked.

'Looking to score, man. There's this guy who drives by in a white van and stops by the park to deal.' Boner tilted his pimply chin toward the suburb's gift to its children, a sad and lonely grassed area.

'What you after? Weed?'

'Nah, man. I'm onto meth now. Fantastic high. No paranoia.' Boner was careful with the last word.

Steven leant on a fence beside Boner. All of his energy vanished. It was like that here. Nothing had changed. Nothing ever would. Even the best of them were trapped, shackled to the place and weary. Those who stayed lied about it. Said things like, 'It may not seem much, but people look out for each other here', which was shit, and 'It takes a bit of time, but once you get to know it, it's in your bones.' Yeah right. It's in your bones, in your veins, in your eyes, your brain.

Boner stiffened, which brought Steven out of himself. A white van crawled down the street. 'You stay here, man. You might spook him, right?' Boner pushed himself off the fence and wandered down the road, trying to look like he was off on a Sunday walk. If Steven were a drug dealer, he thought he would drive straight by, but then the world didn't work that way. It was the poor and illiterate who made up most of a dealer's clientele.

The van motored slowly past the park. Boner continued to lope toward it while appearing to ignore it altogether. Down past Steven's old house it came until it reached the corner, where it crawled to a stop. Boner stopped too. He stared at the van and then turned to Steven with his palms cocked to the sky, a gestural, 'What the fuck?' Steven pushed himself off the fence and strode toward him. Boner put a hand out to slow him and shook his head.

Steven watched him approach the passenger window and knock on the darkened glass. He put his hands onto the glass to cut the glare and peered in. He seemed to take forever and just as Steven was wondering how much there could be to find in the front seat of a two-seater van, Boner reeled back and vomited on the black asphalt. Steven ran toward him then and even before he got to Boner and around to the driver's side to wrench the door open, his mind had cycled through the possibilities.

The driver sat with his head on the wheel. His two hands were still at ten and two as if he had fallen asleep, except in his lap was bits of brain and a bucket load of blood. In the windscreen was a neat, almost invisible, bullet hole where the dealer's head would have been.

'Did you hear anything?' Boner asked, looking around at the houses and into the park for a shooter.

'No. We got to go, Boner. We can't be around this thing. I can't be around this thing.'

But Boner stood still, scanning the park and the houses, like some innocent bystander who just happened by. 'Come on, man.' Steven pulled at his hoodie. Boner started to move toward Steven, now the initial momentum was not up to him, and Steven kept him going with repeated pushes in his skinny back, until they were down the road and around the corner.

'What the fuck?' Boner kept saying over and over. They came to rest on the front stairs of Boner's mother's house. Boner pulled out his smokes and dropped one twice before he could get it between his lips. He hands shook as he brought the lighter flame to its tip.

'Boner, you all right mate?'

He looked up. His face was white. He seemed to be searching for words.

'It's the shock,' Steven said. 'It will pass.'

Boner shook his head. 'Nah, it's not that. I don't know who to go to, man.'

'You don't need to go to anyone. Don't get involved.'

'Nah, that's not it.I don't know who to go to to score, man. He was it.'

Steven heard his panic. He felt it streaming from Boner in a long silent wail. It was a wailing he had been born into, a noise so silent and yet so gripping, other words bounced off. Other tragedies meant nothing.

'I'm going,' Steven said, but Boner didn't hear him. Steven looked back once. Boner was already off down the street in search of another dealer.

HOMELESS

Fiona sat under the enormous tree. The long grass waved before her, obscuring and revealing the fence line, opening and closing like the slow blink of an eye. Visiting here had not been her intention when she'd left the house. She had imagined a kind of celebratory walk. The bullying feature was done, and she knew it was good. The cells in her body had exulted, fizzing along her arms and legs. A jaunt to the creek and back was in order, a kind of skip and bounce down the track, like an under-gravitating astronaut.

Instead, she had been drawn to the tree for the first time since the dead cow day. From where she sat, she could see the rub marks on the bough where the cow had hung. The wood appeared polished and quite beautiful. The patch brought to mind long dining tables set with silver and tall four-poster beds. She was oddly prosaic about dead cows now. The lifeless fox hanging on her front fence was a likely explanation.

The live cows were stand-offish. They tore at the grass and chewed steadily, keeping a baleful eye on her. Occasionally, one would fill its giant lungs with air and fire off a protest.

Fiona pushed the small of her back into the solid trunk. The afternoon had the flavour of an ending. In what way though? An end to the bullying story. An end to her long-standing battles with Hugh. Something had mended between them. He was eager for her opinion again. She prized that above everything, after feeling its lack.

She took in a deep breath and it felt as though it were her first. It was like the breath most treasured after defibrillation. In its gasp, she saw the doctor's bouncing buttocks through the mirror at the B&B, Alick with a dead chicken cupped in his hand, Hugh digging in the garden, Lochie with hope in his eyes and the smallness of herself in the paddock on that first day. These memories startled her like the outcome of a magician's trick. They had been laid down without her knowing it.

The rough bark of the tree rubbed the skin of her lower back where her shirt had ridden up. She placed her hand behind her and felt the groves of the old trunk with her fingers. How long had it stood there? How deep were its roots? Its canopy was a dome above her. Only slices of blue sky showed through. How steadfast, she thought. How fucking marvellous!

***

Steven hadn't left the house all day. The rolling ghost car and the brains on the windshield had thrown him. He jumped at shadows and saw his mother too often, shambling down the hall or pouring shots of vodka in the kitchen. These visions came to him sideways, out of the corner of his eye. It was as if she lived there still, as if they both did. Mostly, he lay on his hiking mat and stared at the spots of mildew on the lounge room ceiling. He knew he had to get out before he was sucked in. One more night, he told himself before drifting off to sleep.

The sound of a key in the lock and the squeaking of hinges woke him. He opened his eyes to find a bald man in a suit standing over him waving his arms. Daylight streamed through the open door.

'What do you think you are doing?' the man shrieked. There was spittle at the corner of his mouth. He turned slightly, 'I'm terribly sorry about this,' he said. A fat man and a thin, weary-looking woman stood behind him. 'This never happens in this neighbourhood,' the agent said.

Steven and the fat man smirked at the obvious lie.

The agent waggled a finger at Steven. 'Now, you just lie there while I ring the police. They will be here quick-smart,' he said to the couple.

'I'm not hanging around for the coppers,' the fat man said, galvanised into action. 'Come on, Crystal.'

The weary woman stared fixedly at the agent. 'Let the boy go,' she said. Her voice was slow and deep.

'I don't know about that,' the agent replied, keying numbers into his mobile phone. 'I have a property to protect.'

Still, the woman glared at him. There was steel in her.

'Come on, Crystal,' urged the fat man from the front door, as he scanned the street for cops.

Crystal didn't move. 'Get your things, boy, and get out of here,' she hissed.

Steven sprung from his mat, collected his stuff, and raced through the open door. He was already around the corner and was taking a short-cut through the swampy land alongside the main road when he realised he had left his tent behind.

*

Fiona studied Lochie in the rear-view mirror. Grief over the chickens had changed him. There was no enthusiastic wave as she pulled up at the bus stop, no struggle with Hugh for the front seat. No tumbling words over the day's events.

'We could get more chickens, couldn't we Mum?' Hugh said into the silence. He was steadfast in his support now.

'We could,' Fiona replied. 'What do you think about that, Lochie?' She watched him in the mirror again.

Lochie said nothing. He turned himself almost sideways on the seat and stared out of the window.

'I've bought Alick a thank-you card for helping us with the chickens,' Fiona said. 'I'd like both of you to write something in it.'

Lochie looked back from the window. Fiona watched him think about it. Then he nodded once and returned his attention to the passing fields.

Back at the house, Fiona retrieved the card from her handbag and took it out onto the verandah. The fox's tail swayed in the breeze. She sat in the old wicker chair and wrote:

> *Dear Alick,*
> *I can't tell how much I appreciate your help in*
> *killing the fox and in helping Hugh, Lochie and I*
> *to bury the chickens. Please let me know if there*
> *is any way I can help you.*
> *Kind regards,*
> *Fiona Lees.*

She took the card back inside and placed it on the table. Hugh came in and wrote something and then Lochie. When they were done, she put the card in its envelope and set off up the track. Over the hill, a black and white cow complained in a small grassy paddock. She peered into the dark corners of the shed looking for Alick but did not see him. The door of the large two-storey brick house was resolutely shut.

Fiona knocked softly and then more loudly. Her phone rang in her pocket and she fished it out. It was Julia. She pressed the power button to silence it and knocked again. There was the sound of a chair scraping across the floor inside and the door was flung open. Alick stood in complete disarray before her. For a second, she thought he was someone else. He was wearing pyjamas, the old kind made of a striped blue and grey flannelette. He had mismatched the buttons on his shirt and his hair stood up on end.

'Are you sick?' she asked him.

'No.'

'Your cow is upset,' she said.

'I need to milk her. Sven used to do it.'

And now he's gone, Fiona thought. 'Did he tell you where he went and why?'

'No,' he replied. Alick smoothed down his hair and pulled his dressing gown closed. She looked away. She knew she had embarrassed him.

'So why are you here?' he asked.

Fiona toyed with the card in her hands. It felt stupid now, but it was too late. 'The boys and I wanted to thank you for helping with the fox and the chickens the other morning. We bought you a card. I know it's not much, but we wanted you to know how grateful we are.'

Alick took the card she offered him. He stared at her, then down at the envelope as if he believed this to be the strangest eventuality. He nodded once and then shut the door.

The image of the dishevelled farmer stayed with Fiona as she walked down the track toward the old farmhouse. She had managed the opposite of what she had intended. She had done him harm with her cheap card.

When she reached her front gate, she turned on her phone. Immediately, it alerted her to her unread messages. The first was from Julia. 'Fi, it's Julia. I want to make sure you are alright. I was wondering if you needed talk about Richard – about everything, really.'

The second one was too. 'I'm sorry, Fiona. I don't mean to be nosy. I just don't know what to do. Please ring me back.'

Fiona heard the catch in Julia's voice.

The third message was from Steph. 'I'd like you to drop in for a chat before the conference on Monday. Ring through to Padma to set it up. She knows what I've got on.'

✻

'Holy fuck, Stevie. They told me you were back. Didn't believe it. I said who would come back to this shit hole, right?' Marius filled the doorway of the house on Wagner Street. The meat on his shoulders and arms looked fit to feed a family. When Steven had last seen him, he was a skinny twenty-year-old sitting on the retaining wall outside, his legs dangling over the edge and his big feet swinging in the breeze. Now, he wrapped one of his arms around Steven's shoulders and the weight of it was immense. 'Come in, cuz,' he said. 'Have a beer with me.'

At least Marius's M.O hadn't changed. He would be so fucking likeable. Shower a bloke with kindness and beer, but all the time be looking for an angle. Steven had vowed to resist; to play it cool. He would say nothing about the dead dealer and, if he was asked, would keep his thoughts about it to himself. The more stand-offish he was, he decided, the more Marius would turn on the charm and perhaps spot him enough money to buy another tent.

Steven dropped his pack inside the front door. 'How's it going? he said.

'Good, good,' Marius nodded, twisting the top of a beer like he was wringing its neck. He passed the bottle to Steven, who had taken a seat on an expensive leather lounge. Marius opened one for himself. 'Business is good,' he said, indicating the quality of his furnishings with a tilt of his beer.

Steven didn't ask what his business was. He didn't want to know.

'So how goes it with you, buddy?' Marius asked, taking a seat across from him in a fancy reclining armchair and offering him his undivided attention.

'It's good. It's good,' Steven replied.

'I heard you stayed a couple of nights at the old place.'

Steven nodded. A fissure opened up in his chest and fear bubbled from it. He had told Boner nothing. Someone had seen him.

'Brought back a few memories, I'm sure,' Marius nodded into his hammy lap.

'Nah,' Steven lied. 'It's just a joint. Nothing special.'

'Right. Right,' Marius nodded, gazing out of the window.

Steven knew something was wrong. Marius was keeping his distance. Steven watched his jaw working beneath the skin of his cheek. Marius seemed on the point of saying something, when his phone rang and startled them both. He stood and, with phone already to his ear, moved off deeper into the house. Steven rose from the sofa and walked quietly after him. He found Marius leaning with his forehead against an enormous pane of glass which took up one wall of a fancy extension.

'Look, it wasn't him,' Marius said, rolling his forehead on the cool glass.

Steven rounded an air hockey table and moved behind a bookcase stuffed with video game cases.

'He's not the type. I've known him since he was a little fella,' Marius said.

'Anyway, he's only just back. He wouldn't even know the lay of the land.'

Marius was silent for time and Steven could hear a muffled voice on the other end of the line. Suddenly, Marius spluttered in disbelief. 'Boner Phillips is a drug-fucked imbecile, who's only trying to score cheap meth.' Marius looked around to see if Steven had overheard him. Steven withdrew further behind the bookcase.

'All right, all right. I'll bring him in, and you can suss him out, but I'm telling you it's a big waste of time.'

Steven heard the last of this as he ran through the house. He scooped up his pack and bolted down the stairs.

A JOB WELL DONE

'We'll be okay, Mum. Come on, Lochie.' Hugh coaxed his little brother out of the car at the bus stop. 'A half an hour isn't long to wait.'

This new compliant Hugh was unfamiliar. It was Lochie who was reluctant. He dragged himself from the car and sat miserably under the shelter.

'Remember, your Grandmother will pick you up from school and I'll collect you later, okay?'

'It's fine, Mum. We've got it,' Hugh said.

Fiona nodded and called out to Lochie, 'See you later tonight, sweetheart.' Lochie didn't acknowledge her.

She needed to help him deal with the death of his chickens, but it would have to wait. There was the meeting with Steph and then the conference. She steered the car onto the road toward the city.

Padma waved her through to Steph's office. 'She is waiting for you.'

'Do you know what this is about?' Fiona asked.

Padma shook her head. 'No idea.'

When Fiona walked into Steph's office it was empty. She stood for a while taking in the amount of paper on the desk. On the walls were production schedules with red crosses and arrows marking changes and work done. A file cabinet with all four drawers ajar stood near the desk, looking like it might topple. Fiona unloaded documents off the visitor's chair and sat. Her mind cycled through the busy day to come. She stood again. She had so much to do.

'Sorry, I think my breakfast bagel was off,' Steph said, sweeping into the room. 'Have spent a half hour on the loo!'

'Oh, right!'

Steph performed a S-shaped move past the filing cabinet and sat. Fiona sat too.

Her editor spread her hands facedown, fingers wide like starfish, on the files in front of her. Then she picked up a pen and fiddled with it. Fiona's stress rose a notch.

'You have done work for me for a long time?' Steph looked to her for confirmation.

Fiona nodded. She waited while Steph did the starfish hands again, wondering if the magazine was going under like so many before it. 'Is there something wrong?'

'God, no! I just wanted to tell you how good your last feature was.'

Fiona felt lightheaded with relief.

'I know I don't often spray it around, but I'm thinking of raising your rate.' She consulted her diary. 'How does $1.10 a word sound?'

Steph reserved this pay rate for industry experts. 'Sure. That sounds great. Thanks.'

'It is well deserved.'

'I really appreciate it, Steph.' Fiona rose to leave. 'Well, I better get ready for the conference. It starts today.'

'Yes, of course.' Steph was fidgeting with the pen again.

'Was there anything else?' Fiona asked.

'Actually, I ran into Richard at a town planning function.' Steph waved the idea of it away from herself. 'I know, normally boring as bat shit, except for one thing.' She raised an eyebrow at Fiona.

Fiona's stomach clenched. 'Jesus, what did he say?'

'A little more than you have lately,' Steph said. 'Look, I know this is none of my business and I'm not at all good at this sort of thing, but I thought you should know.'

'Okay. What did he say?' Fiona asked again.

'When I asked him how he was doing in the country, he looked at me as if I'd had a stroke.'

There was no sound in the room.

Steph continued. 'Turns out you went to the country without him and he doesn't know where you or the kids are.'

Fiona's stomach clenched. 'You didn't tell him where I was, did you?'

'What's to tell? Somewhere with grass and cows. That's all I know,' Steph said. 'If you did tell me, I didn't listen.'

Fiona slumped with relief.

'Look, I know we work together and don't generally socialise, but you are a hermit and have kids and things. Still, I thought you might tell me something this big,' Steph said. 'Instead, I hear it from a righteous bastard I see once a year at the Christmas party.'

Fiona was surprised at the hurt in her voice.

As much as she tried to resist it, Fiona felt a smile coming on. She wasn't the kind to confide. Something always stopped her. Yet, Steph had become her friend anyway. It was nice to know that.

'What are you smiling at?' Steph croaked.

'I'm so sorry. I'm sorry about all of it, but I am so grateful you care,' Fiona said.

Steph grunted and, in her best hard-nosed editor guttural, she said, 'Of course I bloody-well care.'

'Right,' Fiona said.

'Anyway, so what I'm guessing is that Richard is a bit of a bastard and you've run off into the bush to escape him. Is that right?'

Fiona kept her face deadpan. 'Pretty much.'

Steph stood at her desk. 'Well, I'm glad we've sorted that out.' Steph glared toward the door. 'And, Padma, you can come in now.'

Fiona heard an intake of breath and the click of a heel before Padma entered the room.

Steph took hold of her computer mouse and her screen came to life. 'We all have work to do,' she said, pointedly to Padma. To Fiona, she said, 'And you've got a conference to get to.'

✳

Alick sat at his dining room table with the thank-you card before him. He read Fiona's message again and then the older boy, Hugh's:

What an awesome shot! Thanks.

The smaller boy's message crouched in the corner of the card:

It was all my fault. I forgot to shut the door. I'm sorry.

'You will only forget once, lad,' Alick muttered. He rose and grabbed the keys to his truck. His next job required a trip into town for the tie wire he needed to mend the fences.

Alick took the bottom track past the old farmhouse, instead of slipping out through the top gate. This route took him past Sven's old campsite. For a few seconds, he could see into the gully behind the ridge as he drove along. The brown square left by the boy's tent was less brown. New grass was growing. Alick turned away and drove over the crest and past the old farmhouse. The place looked empty. The woman's car was gone. He caught sight of the disturbed earth beneath the pepper tree and thought of the little boy. He guessed him to be eleven or twelve. A tough age. He'd done a lot of learning about life back then – about death, about responsibility – but there was so much more learning to come. It made him tired to think on it.

Driving out of the gate and accelerating onto the main road cleared his head. He set the old truck at the hill and pushed it forward. The engine growled and the chassis vibrated. 'Come on, you old bastard!' Alick cried through the open window into the cool breeze. The truck crested the hill and plunged down the other side. Alick whooped like a boy.

He was pink-cheeked when he pulled to a stop outside the produce store. Jim was yanking at some promotional bunting around his hay bales.

'Alick,' he said with a quick nod.

Alick stood and examined the hay. 'Do you tell your customers there's very little good lucerne in them, Jim? Mostly straw, I'd say.'

'Shut up, Alick,' Jim snapped. 'A man's got to make a living.' Jim tied off the last of the bunting and followed Alick into the store. 'What can I do you for?'

'I'm wanting some tie wire and a pair of snips,' Alick said. 'A good ten metres of the stuff should do me.'

'Righto, then. I keep it out the back. Come on.'

Alick followed Jim through the shop and over the wooden walkway which spanned a trench left over before the back extension was put on in 1985. Alick could be sure of the year. That was the time of the big flood.

The sun blinded him as they walked outside.

'This way,' Jim said. Alick followed along the back of the shed past a cage of chickens and toward a pile of fence posts and looped sections of different gauge wires. Jim reached up into the shelving and brought down a tight loop of pliable wire. 'Will this do you?' Jim asked.

Alick nodded. 'I'll have a half a dozen of those chickens there too,' he said.

Jim looked at the cage of flapping birds and back to Alick. 'You sure?'

'Of course I'm bloody sure,' Alick replied.

Jim shuffled off to get some boxes and Alick stood outside the pen. He chose a big flouncy hen a little older than the others. Good to have one with some smarts, he thought. The rest could come from younger stock.

✳

Exhaust fumes floated over Steven from the nearby intersection. He turned away. His two close calls with Marius and the real estate agent had wearied him. When he could go no further, he rolled out his hiking mat under a shady tree on the edge of an empty baseball park. The urge to lie down and sleep was strong. He was more than tired though. A sob shuddered through him and he bit his lip.

Inside his chest, a balloon inflated and pressed on his breast bone. It solidified into a hard ball of loss. Without his tent, he was homeless.

'You know you can't stay here.'

A shadow passed over him. Steven opened his eyes. A man in a caretaker's uniform stood over him. A fat tear crawled from the corner of Steven's eye.

The man crouched beside him. 'Hey, are you okay?'

Steven sat up, but beyond that he had no idea what to do.

'Are you a traveller?' the man asked, looking at Steven's pack.

Steven shook his head.

'Are you hungry?'

Steven nodded.

'Well, follow me.'

The caretaker strode off toward a club house. Steven struggled to his feet and gathered what was left of his belongings.

'The wife always packs me too much. She's Italian,' the man said, when they were sitting under the verandah with their backs against the rough bricks of the club house. 'I hope you like meatball sandwiches.'

Steven nodded and took the offered sandwich. Both of them chewed steadily, looking out over the green grass of the baseball diamond.

'Where are you from, if you don't mind me asking?'

Steven turned his head and looked at the man. He had short grey hair and a bristling moustache poking out from under his nose. His skin was as sun-toughened as Alick's. 'I used to be from Woodridge.'

The caretaker shook his head and looked at Steven. 'Well, I never. Just down the road, hey? I would have sworn you were from someplace else.'

The man poured milky tea from his thermos and gave Steven a cup. They drank in silence. When they were done, the caretaker took both cups to a tap hanging off the clubhouse wall and rinsed them. Steven watched as he replaced the lunch things back into a small esky. When he was finished, he sat again beside Steven. 'I don't mean to pry,' he said, 'but do you have anywhere to go?'

The green of the baseball diamond spread out before him and the air cleared for a moment. He saw the old man and Harry standing out by the BBQ and Daisy with her soft brown eyes. He saw Lochie with the chicken in his lap and Hugh placing a piece of wood on the chopping block for Steven to split. He imagined a room at the top of Alick's house with a window and maybe a desk.

'I do,' Steven nodded. 'If they still want me around.'

'Well, there's no harm in asking,' the caretaker said. 'No harm at all.'

*

'So, what you are asking me is, why is a bloke a specialist in gender inequality? Is that right?' Gordon Watts sat across from Fiona in a bar near the convention centre. On his necktie were crumbs from the potato chips he had been eating and there was something benignly shambolic about him.

'I suppose I am,' Fiona said, smiling.

Watts stared into his scotch glass. 'To tell you the truth, I'm probably as inappropriate as the next man and only slightly better at hiding it. I didn't start out studying gender. I was, and still am, interested in inequalities of any kind. It's the media which has pigeon-holed me more than anything.'

'How so?'

'I was asked to comment some years back about the disparity in wages between men and women in the US. I had some data from a study which looked at wider inequalities but, as it turned out, the story the press chose to focus on was gender.'

'Did that annoy you?' Fiona knew she was baiting him.

He smiled. 'No, not at all. If my data can help, then it should.'

Fiona smiled back. Gordon Watts was a savvy interviewee, though a slightly drunk one, she suspected. 'Can I ask you when your study was carried out?'

'That was back in 2009,' Watts replied, waggling a finger at the bartender for another scotch.

'Do you think much has changed since then?' Fiona asked.

'I'd like to say yes, but I don't know. It seems to me a lot of the social mores which existed back then are still around today. To see change, I think we would need to look at a much longer timeframe – a generation perhaps. How was it for your mother or mine, for example?'

Fiona had already put her notebook away since the official part of the interview was over. 'Would it be okay if I took that down?' she said.

Watts nodded and sipped from his refreshed glass. The amber fluid glowed in the soft lighting of the backlit bar. Watts cupped the glass in his two hands and the glow disappeared.

'Do you think generational change is good enough?' she asked him.

He looked into the glass. 'Of course, I don't,' he said, turning to her, 'but remember I'm little more than a statistician.'

Fiona heard the weariness in his voice, frustration perhaps, exhaustion, drunkenness. 'Life hurts,' she said, picking up her bag.

He lifted his head again and considered her. 'Yes, it does.'

'Well, thank you for your time, Mr Watts,' she said, 'but I need to be getting on. I have to pick up my sons.'

Watts placed his glass on the bar and held out his hand. 'It's been a pleasure, slightly depressing, but still a pleasure,' he said, shaking her hand. 'If you ever need some comment, just send me an email,' he said.

The light outside the front door shone like a beacon, just as it had done so many years ago when Fiona would return home late from parties. It drew her in and her hand reached for door handle and found it locked. She took a key out of her bag and opened the door. Julia stood in the hall, as if waiting for her.

'I just wanted to see you,' she whispered.

Fiona realised how disorientating all of this was for Julia. 'You know I can't talk about this here.' She inclined her head toward the sitting room at the end of the hall. 'I hope you haven't told them.'

'Of course, I haven't. I just–' Julia put an arm around her. 'I just need you to know how sorry I am. I should have helped. I should have known.'

'I was very good at hiding it, Jules,' Fiona said, walking down the hall with her sister beside her.

Julia pulled at her arm to stop her and she began to cry. 'But I'm your older sister and now Mum and Dad are really weird about the child custody thing and that's on me.'

Fiona's throat swelled and it hurt to swallow. 'You have been the best oldest sister anyone could have, and I love you. You have looked after me my entire life, but you need to back off and leave this to me. Okay?' Fiona stared into Julia's tear-streaked face. 'Okay?'

Julia nodded.

'Right. You go wash your face and I'll get the boys ready for home.'

Both her parents greeted her with tight lips when she entered the living room.

'Hello, darling,' her father said, rising from his armchair and leaning against the mantle. 'How was the conference?'

'Fine, Dad. How were the boys? No trouble, I hope?'

'They are never any trouble, dear,' Gwendolyn said, remaining seated. Her words were heavily weighted.

'Say what you mean to say, Mum, before I go and wake the boys,' Fiona said, perching on the arm of her father's chair.

Her mother sighed. 'Well, it seems there is little we can say. You are determined to destroy your marriage and the futures of your children.' She sniffed and looked away.

Fiona was nonplussed. 'How am I destroying my children's futures, Mum? Tell me. How?'

Her mother looked across to Fiona's father and then at Fiona. 'All right, I will tell you. Everyone knows children are best raised by two parents. No matter what the problems in the marriage, the mother and father need to be there together.' Gwendolyn's voice was shrill.

It was on the tip of Fiona's tongue to tell her mother the whole truth, but she heard Gordon Watts's voice in her mind, as clearly as if she were sitting with him at the bar. How was it for your mother and mine? And this stilled her tongue. One day, she might tell them, when she was free of everything. But not yet.

DARK MATTER

Fiona and Hugh stood before the chicken pen staring at the new hens.

'Alick must have bought them,' Fiona whispered.

It was Hugh who noticed them first, when he came out to work in the garden.

'Shall I go and get Lochie?' he asked.

Fiona nodded. She watched the chickens scratch in the dark soil. One was bigger than the rest and the others followed her. Fiona smiled. Of course, Alick would know such things. Something white fluttered in the laying boxes in the back corner of the pen. She walked around the back of the pen and opened the latch. She reached in and withdrew a piece of paper. On it was the most beautiful handwriting Fiona had ever seen. It read: Mistakes are how we learn.

Tears pricked at the corner of her eyes. Of course, she thought. The old man had understood what she could not. Lochie was sick with guilt.

Fiona heard the screen door scrape open and the sound of Lochie and Hugh approaching from around the side of the house.

'I don't want a surprise,' Lochie was muttering as they drew closer. 'This is stupid.'

Suddenly, he stopped. Fiona saw his back stiffen. 'I don't want them,' he said. 'You shouldn't have bought them.'

'I didn't,' Fiona said. 'Alick did.' She handed Lochie the note.

She watched him swallow a lump in his throat as he read Alick's message. A pact had been made between them; of that she was certain. Perhaps there was room for another.

✳

Alick was milking Daisy when he heard the rumble of Harry's four-wheel drive. He peered over his shoulder, his hands still working, as Harry drove around the shed and pulled to a stop beside the house paddock. Alick went back to watching the milk foam in the bucket.

'Hello, old man,' Harry called, jumping down from the driver's seat.

Alick nodded and kept on milking. He had an inkling about Harry's visit and it did not please him.

'So, how's everything going?' Harry asked, leaning a leg on a lower fence rail.

'It's fine,' Alick said without turning. 'The spring rain is not far off. I can feel it.'

'Right. I don't doubt you,' Harry said looking at the sky. 'So, is there anything that needs doing?'

'Nope. There's fencing, but I like to do that myself.'

'Just thought I'd come and see how you are going since … well, you know.' Harry cleared his throat at the end of this.

Alick withdrew the bucket from beneath Daisy and Harry was through the gate quickly to take it from him.

'How is Daisy?' he asked, giving her a pat on the flank.

'She's fine,' Alick said.

Harry ran a hand along the length of her with the bucket slopping about in his other hand. 'She's getting on now isn't she?'

Alick stood up from the stool and took a moment to adjust his balance. 'Nope, she bloody isn't. You'd have her down at the meat works quick-smart, I'm sure,' he replied.

Harry shook his head. 'No, no. You know I wouldn't,' the vet said, taking his own offence.

Alick did know this. 'Do you want a cuppa?'

'Sure,' Harry said.

They walked to shed, Harry with the milk and Alick with the stool.

'Take a bit off the top for tea,' Alick said to Harry nodding toward the jug which stood on top of the shed fridge, 'and chill the rest for later.'

'Sure thing,' Harry said. 'Not often you get milk like this these days.'

Alick walked to the house with Harry. He'd known the vet for a long time. Must be going on twenty years, he thought. Still, it didn't give him the right to meddle.

Alick was in the kitchen boiling the jug when Harry finally came out with it. 'Do you ever think of retiring, Alick?' he called through the doorway.

'Nope,' Alick replied, bringing the cups of tea to the table.

Harry looked around at the walls, the furniture, the space, 'Don't you get lonely here all by yourself?'

'Nope.'

'Okay, then,' Harry said, draining his teacup and rising from his chair. 'I guess I'd better get on with my day.'

Alick was walking Harry to his car, when he saw Fiona and Hugh coming around the side of the shed. Harry saw them too.

Fiona waved. Alick waved back, uncomfortable under Harry's scrutiny. He cleared his throat. 'It's the woman and one of the lads from the old farmhouse.'

'Right,' Harry said, watching them approach.

Alick studied his boots. 'Her name's Fiona. The boy's Hugh.'

Fiona and Hugh were close now. She nodded to Harry and Alick introduced them both. Hugh stood off to the side.

'We were very surprised to find chickens in the pen this morning and I was wondering whether you might be responsible for that,' Fiona said.

Alick nodded.

'Well, thank you. I didn't think Lochie would smile again. You are a good man, Alick.'

'I expect eggs when they lay,' Alick said, nodding to Hugh.

Fiona smiled. 'Of course. As many as you want, but we have another proposition for you. Hugh?'

The boy stepped forward then and cleared his throat, nervously. 'Could you teach me to milk your cow?'

Alick was genuinely surprised. He shot a glance toward Harry and knew he was also. 'So, why would I do that then?' Alick asked him.

The boy went pale and stammered, 'I want to work outside and I could help around the place. I wouldn't expect you to pay me anything – at least not to begin with.'

'I wouldn't be soft on you. I'm tough,' Alick said.

'So am I,' the boy said straight-backed, and by the look of him, Alick didn't doubt it.

Harry let out a big booming laugh. 'Well, I never. I'm sure the old man needs the help, even though he would never tell you that.'

'Shut up, Harry,' Alick snapped.

'It's not charity, Harry,' Fiona said. 'Hugh is thinking of working on the land and he needs someone to teach him.'

'Like an apprentice?' Harry said.

'Yes, just like that,' Fiona replied.

Alick nodded. 'In that case, meet me at the home paddock at dawn tomorrow. Daisy waits for no man.'

❀

Late that night, Fiona threw the kitchen scraps from dinner to the new chickens. She could barely make out their huddled forms. One chicken let out a disgruntled cluck at the disturbance. 'Sorry,' she whispered. She checked the wire door once again. That day, she and Lochie had checked it many times.

Inside, all was silent. Hugh had gone to bed early and Lochie had drifted off into his room with a serious face and his pact with Alick to consider.

She sat at her computer and wrote quickly. Watts's statistics were discouraging. Change seemed a long way off. She thought of the man at the bar with crumbs on his tie and the glass of whiskey in his hand. Was he always to be the bearer of bad news? Was she?

She wrote on: 'What do these statistics reveal of the lives of working women? Wages are unequal and thinly-veiled sexual harassment is still present in many workplaces. A woman, who speaks her mind, can still be perceived as an annoyance or a pretender to power, rather than someone who is exercising her right to voice her ideas.

Fiona knew her language was strong. Perhaps it was too strong for *In Business*, but let Steph tell her so. Her confidence had grown since the success of her last story and maybe she had earned the right to speak plainly.

These statistics do not stand alone. They speak to the core problem of systemic inequality, the dark matter which has governed the lives of working women. Fiona pulled back from her keyboard. Her blood was up. She knew she could go on, but she would end it there.

She opened a new file and continued to write. What followed was for herself. Statistics can't explain the lives full of careful allowances given to men by women in exchange for their safety. That is a pact too and girls are born into this ugly status-quo. She saved the document and was prompted for a file name. The cursor blinked. In a flurry, she typed: Book

Gently, she closed down her laptop and placed it on the coffee table. She needed sleep. Her body felt so heavy that she pulled a blanket over herself and curled up where she was on the sofa.

✻

Steven slipped through the streets toward the train station. He passed his old house, its windows like blind eyes. He thought of the tent he had left behind, but he knew it would be already gone, thrown in a skip somewhere out of spite. Since he had decided to return to the farm, he didn't care. Stepping back from this decision was now impossible. A tremor ran through him. What would he do if Alick said no?

Boner Phillips stepped from a darkened side street so suddenly, he almost collided with him. Once Steven had regained his equilibrium and Boner his nonchalance, Boner leaned in close.

'So, where are you off to, Stevie boy?'

Steven pulled back and repositioned the shoulder straps of his pack. 'I'm out of here,' he answered. He knew Boner had dropped him in it and could not be trusted.

'Where too, though?' Boner asked, hiking his jeans up around his skinny arse and cocking his head toward the pack.

'I'm off up north,' Steven lied. 'Gonna get some work on the tourist boats out to the reef.'

Boner's eyes went wide. Leaving the neighbourhood was beyond him. Steven realised Boner knew nothing of the world.

'Well, I have to get going,' Steven said. He threw in another lie, just in case. 'Gotta bus to catch.' Steven stepped around Boner and continued on his way.

'Hey, Stevie boy! I've got a message for you from the lads,' he called after him.

Steven turned back to Boner. He saw him pull a gun from the back of his jeans. He felt the bullet as a punch in his chest. It knocked him over and face-down onto the footpath. That Boner could fire a gun and hit him astonished him. He blinked furiously. Before him was the house where he and his mother had lived. He closed his eyes. He had not meant to die here.

ANOTHER FOX

When Alick couldn't sleep, he walked the paddocks. He inherited the compulsion from his father. He thought of him now. The tug of guilt was less these days. Then, he thought of Sven. Alick was no older than the lad when he had taken himself off to Vietnam. Youth had no foresight. It was as hard to be young as it was to be old, Alick thought. Perhaps his father had understood that. He liked to think so.

He passed the old farmhouse, its windows dark beneath the brow of the verandah. He turned off the track toward Sven's old campsite. No one would know it now, he realised. What was left of the fire had been dispersed by animals looking for scraps of food. The brown patch of grass had filled in with green.

He climbed to the top of the ridge and looked down toward the creek. A raindrop hit his shoulder and ran down his oilskin coat. The moon passed in and out of the clouds and the edges of the trees down by the creek were dark against the sky.

Alick set off across the paddock toward the creek and the road beyond it. He counted the steers in a patch of moonlight and nodded to himself. Then, he moved on through the long grass. Near the trees bordering the creek where fat raindrops crackled on dead leaves, he heard another sound. Alick slipped into the trees and waited. His rifle rose up and found its familiar place against his cheek. He waited for another patch of open sky. The rustling started again and he focussed his sight on where he knew the track to be. With each new sound, he adjusted his sight further, waiting for the moon. The footsteps grew louder. There was no mistaking the sound. Two feet, not four, dragging through dead leaves. He stood as still as the trees around him until the sound receded. The moon shone through the parted clouds and Alick saw a figure walking along the track. Alick left the trees and fell into step behind him.

※

Fiona started up from the sofa. She shrugged off her sleep and she strained to listen beyond the walls of the house toward the chicken pen. There it was, a rustling, the sound of scratching on metal.

'Right, you little bastard,' she muttered. She reached for her jacket, grabbed the torch from the kitchen, and shoved her feet into her rubber boots by the back door.

As she stepped out into the night, true rain began to fall. The damp earth smelt of field mushrooms and rainforest floors. Fiona listened carefully, but all sound was drowned by the fat drops on the iron roof. She lifted the hood of her jacket and stepped beyond the awning into the sodden yard. The shovel stood upright in the vegetable garden, but she had no faith in it. This time, the element of surprise was all she could hope for.

Fiona kept to the shadows of the pepper tree as she closed in on the chicken pen. Her grip on the unlit torch was fierce. She squinted into the enclosure and pressed the switch. Two chickens stood up on spindly legs and gave off indignant squawks. The remaining four turned their eyes away and huddled together under the cover of the nesting boxes. Even so, Fiona swung the torch beam into the furthest corners of the pen, searching for cruel yellow eyes. The two chickens kept up their murmuring. 'Sorry, girls,' she whispered, as she checked the door of the pen once again and turned off the torchlight. Immediately, the hens settled down onto their perches.

The rain lessened as she stood watching the sleeping chickens and her eyes accustomed themselves to the dark. She looked up to the sky. The moon shone dimly through its covering of cloud. The wings of a fruit bat beat overhead as it flew low across the sky. Only a few drops fell on her now from the leaves of the trees overhead. Fiona stood still. She felt the night world around her, through her skin, in her nostrils and on the tip of her tongue. A frog began its deep crackling call somewhere up in the guttering. She smiled. Almost certainly, it was the noise which had woken her. This was when she heard the creak of footsteps on the front stairs to the verandah. The frog in the guttering called out again.

✳

Alick took up his position under the large fig tree across from the old farmhouse. He put his old joints to work until he was prone with the rifle barrel resting on a curved buttress root.

He pulled up the collar of his oilskin and became part of the ground around him. His breathing slowed and shallowed to featherlight and his muscles tensed and relaxed of their own accord. Alick pointed his scope on the man's back and made his adjustments as he mounted the stairs to the front verandah. The check of his shirt came into focus. Alick didn't know who he was. He didn't need a story. There was only the man, the lessening rain, the degree of light, and a slight breeze from left to right. He focussed on the man's hand as he opened the screen door outward. Across the space between them, Alick heard the creaking of hinges.

The man paused on the threshold.

Alick felt the breeze pick up ever so slightly since the rain had stopped and he made his adjustments accordingly.

❋

Fiona crossed the yard to the corner of the house. She crept around to where the verandah met the house and peered between the rails. A dark figure stood holding the screen door open. Her stomach pitched and fell. She needed no more information. She knew it was Richard. Her body grew clammy inside the rain jacket. She didn't move. Cloud thinned over the moon and there was enough light to show his face. She shrunk back around the corner, with her back pressed up against the side of the house. Her need to hide pulled at her. She could disappear in the night and he would never find her. If she took the track back up the hill, she could lose him in Alick's outbuildings. But Hugh and Lochie were inside the house.

Fiona edged around the corner to see Richard place a hand on the doorknob and begin to turn it. She crossed the garden silently while his back was turned and centred herself on the path in the front garden.

'Hello, Richard,' she said.

He turned, letting the screen door fall closed behind him and peered at her.

'What do you want?' Fiona watched him frown, confused by the outline of the bulky coat. She stepped out into the open beyond the shadow made by the house.

Richard studied her, his lip curling. 'So, this is where you've ended up,' he said. 'I must say I'm surprised. I never took you for a country type.'

He said this as if he knew her still.

'Why are you here?'

He walked casually to the steps and sat down on the uppermost one.

Fiona's unease grew.

With his elbows on his knees, he leaned forward and in an exaggerated whisper he said, 'You know why I'm here, Fiona.'

She looked into his eyes and she saw the fox again. 'You like to inflict pain. You're sick,' she hissed.

Richard sucked in a deep breath and he shook his head. 'You always did play the victim. Overly dramatic, is what I think she said.' He tilted his chin and considered the moon. 'Yes, that was it.'

Fiona knew he was drawing her in, but she needed to know. 'Was it my mother who told you where I was?'

It was Fiona's turn to see the theatre in him. He cupped his hand under his chin, propped his elbow on his knee and nodded, observing her carefully. This newest cut was surgical.

'Well,' Fiona said without emotion, 'she doesn't know you like I do.' She made a point of gazing up beyond the roof of the verandah, as if the conversation wasn't enough to hold her attention. Fiona heard the stair creak as he stood up and returned to the front door. 'Why don't you come up here so we can talk?' he asked.

'Why don't you tell me what you want instead?' she asked.

Richard gestured to the screen door. 'We could sit down like adults and discuss things.'

'I don't think so,' Fiona said. 'You may have fooled my mother, but you don't fool me. I know who and what you are.'

'All right, then,' Richard's voice was cold now. 'I received your lawyer's letter about custody. It was hardly respectful.' Richard walked across the verandah, as if to access the house. 'How long did you think you could keep them from me?' he asked, over his shoulder.

She knew he wanted her to follow him, but she held firm. 'Indefinitely,' she said. 'We both know you don't want custody.'

Richard's hand was poised over the doorknob.

Fiona knew she was right. Slowly and purposefully, Richard strode back down the stairs toward her and away from Lochie and Hugh. The slap, when it came, wrenched her head sideways and sent her staggering across the path.

❋

Alick had picked Fiona out of the shadows before she left the protection of the house. Stay there, he had willed her, but she had shown herself. Worse still, she had moved into Alick's line of sight and, just as he was considering another vantage point, the moon floated out from beneath the clouds. The scene flashed in the rifle scope. He watched them talk, but could not hear them. The man walked from the door and sat on the step. Then he moved back to the door with his hand on the knob. Alick's finger moved closer to the trigger. It hovered between the guard and the tightly sprung slither of metal. With the help of the moonlight, he made out the shape of the man's head beneath the verandah and he centred his crosshairs. Alick caught the flicker of movement, the blur of an arm before the woman lurched sideways. The man stood in front of him, free and clear. Alick stilled himself. He blinked once and the world slowed down. He adjusted his aim and fired once and then again into the ridge above him.

❀

'What the fuck!'

From where Fiona lay in the shadows beyond the path, she saw Richard spin wildly looking for the shooter.

'What the fuck, Fiona?' His voice was shrill.

He squinted to see her in the shadows.

'Who is here?' he yelled at her. 'Who has a gun?'

But Fiona didn't answer. She didn't have time to. The door of the old farmhouse flew open and Hugh appeared on the top step with Lochie close behind him. Fiona watched Hugh take in the scene and launch himself off the top step onto his father. The punch he delivered to Richard's stomach took the wind out of him. Hugh had time to throw two more to his father's face before Richard grabbed his arms.

'So, you want to fight now, do you?' Richard asked. 'I'd say it was about time you stood up for yourself.'

Hugh squared up to his father, as Fiona always knew he would. 'No, Hugh,' she moaned, through her aching jaw.

'Hugh!' Lochie screamed.

Father and son came together again. They wrestled across the garden, until Richard freed one arm. He didn't hold back. He drove his fist into Hugh's stomach, the weight of it lifting him from the ground. Fiona saw him crumple. The shovel was in her hands without thought. She held it like a cricket bat, and she swung it. The shovel caught Richard on the hip. He bent double and fell on the path.

'You bitch!' Richard bellowed.

'Go to the boy, Fiona. He won't get up again,' Alick said, standing by the gate. 'Go!'

Fiona ran to Hugh and Lochie. 'Are you okay?'

'My ribs hurt,' Hugh groaned.

'Lochie, get my phone.'

Lochie ran up the stairs, grabbed her phone and brought it down to her. They stayed like that – Hugh on the ground, with Fiona and Lochie beside him, and Alick with his rifle trained on Richard. They stayed there until the police and ambulance arrived.

A WALKING STICK

'Well, that's it then. You have full custody,' her lawyer said. 'And, from what I hear, I don't think you will have any trouble getting a restraining order. The police have filed for one on your behalf. It's up to him to honour it though.'

'He will,' Fiona said.

Lynda Hopper looked up from her papers. 'Are you sure? Some men are not deterred. It motivates them further.'

'Not Richard. What he did, he did secretly. That's the way he needs it to be.'

The lawyer looked down at her hands resting on Fiona's file. 'Butter wouldn't melt in his mouth, right?'

Fiona nodded.

Hopper focussed on writing up her file.

Fiona cleared her throat.

The lawyer raised her head. 'Is there anything else?'

'Yes. I would like to begin divorce proceedings and start on the property settlement.'

Lynda Hopper smiled and Fiona knew the smile was genuine.

'You are doing the right thing,' she said, leaning over the desk to pat Fiona's hand.

'Thanks,' Fiona said. 'Well, I better go. I need to pick up Hugh and Lochie.'

The lawyer stood and came around her desk to walk her out. They shook hands at the door. 'Shall I make an appointment for this time next week?'

'Yes, I'll see you then.'

Out on the street, people hurried along the footpaths. She joined them.

*

Alick leaned on his walking stick as he watched Fiona's car crawl up the track. The stick was something new he was trying. It was lighter than the rifle and purpose-built. The sky above him was a deep blue and the grass vivid green now the spring rain had come. The world smelled fresh again.

Alick flicked a blowfly away from the corner of his eye, as Hugh and Lochie emerged from the car. They ran up the front steps and were inside before their mother had turned off the engine. Alick knew they would be swimming in the waterhole soon. He could wander down and join them there, teach them a thing or two about skipping stones. Fiona stepped out of the car and spotted him on the ridge. She waved to him and Alick smiled.

* * *

Acknowledgments

Thank you to Ellie Gleeson, who is a fine editor and helped me make sense of my story. Likewise to Jennifer Zabinskas, thank you for your attention to detail and moral support.

Many thanks to the Queensland Writers Centre.
I hope you guys (past and present) know how instrumental you are in the development of Queensland writers. All of us are in your debt.

To my petite party of unpaid proofreaders, Kerry Bell, Patrick Pollock, Jacqueline Blondell and Clare Pollock, many thanks.

To my family and my partner, thank you for putting up with me. I think it is fair to say that your jobs were hardest.

About the Author

A writer of short stories, a book reviewer and a novelist, Gabrielle spends half her time on a small property near Tamborine Mountain and the rest living on a boat in Queensland's Moreton Bay. She has worked as a journalist for twenty years. *Numb* is her first published novel. Gabrielle may be contacted through her publisher at heyhomosapiens@gmail.com.

www.ingramcontent.com/pod-product-compliance
Lightning Source LLC
Chambersburg PA
CBHW020141120726
47903CB00007B/2358

9 780648 879008